LEFT BY THE SIDE OF THE ROAD

CHARACTERS WITHOUT A NOVEL

2nd edition

Carolyn P. Schriber

Published by Katzenhaus Books
P.O Box 1629
Cordova, TN 38088-1629

Cover Design by Avalon Graphics

ISBN: 0984592830
ISBN-13: 9780984592838

Library of Congress Control Number: 2013913558
Katzenhaus Books Cordova, TN

"Whenever you feel an impulse to perpetuate a piece of exceptionally fine writing, obey it—whole-heartedly—and delete it before sending your manuscripts to press. Murder your darlings."
—Sir Arthur Quiller-Couch

Contents

Preface

Left by the Side of the Road is a collection of short stories about my darlings and about life in South Carolina's Low Country during the Civil War. It is not a continuous novel, or even a novella, although I have tried to maintain some chronological order among the stories. There is no single plot or story line. The collection is simply that—a series of glimpses into the past.

The characters are real historical figures. They include slaves who were abandoned when the plantation owners fled in fear of the invading Union Army, government officials charged with the logistics of organizing captured territory, Army officers and the women who accompanied them, and abolitionists determined to prove that former slaves could become productive citizens.

Some of these people have appeared in *A Scratch with the Rebels* and *Beyond All Price*. Others make cameo appearances in *The Road to Frogmore*. All of them are here because they share certain characteristics. They are fascinating people in their own right, but they do not play a major role in the novels where they first appeared. Their stories are important in other contexts but not in their original setting. They are characters who were literally "left by the side of the road" as my historical novels developed.

I killed off the unnecessary characters, but they continued to haunt me. And what was I to do with the corpses? Their stories ended up here, not because they are untrue but simply because they had been distractions from the main story line.

Part One: Cuttings from Nellie's Story

Nellie's novel went though several complete revisions. At one time it was titled *Nellie's Wars*; at another, *No Place for a Lady*. Eventually we settled on *Beyond All Price*, but not until the book had undergone drastic changes of emphasis and structure.

Just as I had written what I thought was the final chapter, I made a genealogical discovery that invalidated the last quarter of the book. Here's what happened. From the beginning I knew that there was not much first-hand evidence of Nellie's life, but I trusted my research skills to turn up the facts I needed. It was harder than I expected. In my first searches for Nellie's family, I discovered that there were some 174 women named Nellie Chase, or some derivative thereof, who had been born in the 1830s in Maine and who were still alive during the Civil War. Which one was the one I wanted?

Eventually I was able to narrow my choices down to two individuals. One was born near Bangor, grew up in a family of boys, disappeared from the records in 1860, re-emerged in Nashville in 1864, married a man in Tennessee, settled in

Kentucky, and then disappeared again, this time for good. The other was born in Saco, Maine, in a family with one sister, disappeared from the records in 1860, re-emerged in Baltimore at the end of the war, married a well-known lawyer from Saco, and returned to her hometown to live out her life with a large and happy family whose lives I could trace well into the twentieth century. With little else to guide me, I had to make a choice, and I gambled on the Nellie from Saco.

I was happy with my choice until the day I received an e-mail from a Civil War buff who knew I was working with the Roundhead Regiment. He thought I might be interested in a newspaper clipping he had just discovered in an on-line archive:

DEATH OF NELLIE CHASE

Many brave men in the Union army remember Nellie Chase, the hospital nurse whose untiring devotion cheered the sick and wounded, and no doubt helped to save many lives. In the earlier part of the war she was with the Twelfth Pennsylvania (three months) and afterwards with the One Hundredth, better known as "Roundheads." Following this she was stationed in the hospitals at Nashville. After the war she married Captain W. C. Ernst, and was residing at Paris, Tenn., when the fever broke out. With the old-time heroic spirit still moving her, she nursed the stricken people until last week, when she was attacked with the plague and died at Louisville, where she was taken. Her husband, Captain Ernst, who went into the army with the Fifteenth Pennsylvania (Anderson) Cavalry from Philadelphia, died two days after his wife.

The article had appeared in the Reading, Pennsylvania *Daily Eagle* dated October 13, 1878. Further checking confirmed that this was the Roundheads' Nellie. Her husband's name had been misspelled in the article, but the burial records at the Cave Hill Cemetery in Louisville established him as George W. Ernest. Further searches in various genealogy websites turned up his service record, his employment with the L & N Railroad in Paris, Tennessee, her service under General Rosecrans in Nashville, and their marriage license. I couldn't avoid facing the facts. I had a book that needed to be re-written.

Originally I had intended to have Nellie narrate her story herself, interspersing her own reflections with third-person chapters that she was writing for her granddaughter's benefit. Those interludes were some of my favorite pieces of writing because they seemed to capture the character's innermost thoughts. They worked well until I learned that Nellie had never had a granddaughter, or even any children. There went my entire structure for the novel.

The following selections contain several of the first-person interludes that represent Nellie's thoughts at various early stages of the novel. Five chapters that represent the alternative ending that I discarded in deference to the facts follow them.

Preserving the Memory

Snowfalls are like memories. They hide the ugliness of everyday experiences and soften the edges of our world. They quiet the normal hustle and bustle of life, and because of their very coldness, they make us feel warmer and cozier when we observe them from a safe distance.

I've been sitting here staring out at the street beyond my house. Nothing is moving out there, not even a lonely horse and carriage. The tall pine trees are beginning to bend a bit with the weight of the snow puffs perched on their needles. The gaslights in the house across the way are flickering more than usual—an effect caused by the thickening curtain of snowflakes that separates us. Winter storms on the coast of Maine can be ferocious at times, but this evening the snowfall is gentle.

I've been thinking about memories a lot lately. Perhaps Christmas seasons lead everyone to reminisce a bit about childhood, families, happy times and sad times, surprises and disappointments. This year, though, my memories have a more intense flavor because we are coming to the end of a century. Oh, I know enough history to understand that time is a human invention. When 1899 gives way to the first day of the twentieth century tomorrow, nothing much will actually change. The sun will set and come up again. We'll all be just one day older, and all the same joys and sorrows will color the way we view our world.

The proponents of *fin de siècle* excitement encourage us to look forward to a bright and shining new world. Undreamed-of opportunities, untold advances in every endeavor, solutions to all the world's problems are only a date away. Or so they would have us believe. But the changes, I suspect, will be no more substantial than those snow puffs adorning my pine trees. When the first wind blows through, they'll disintegrate, filtering through the branches to make dispirited little mounds on the lawn, and leaving the sharpness of the needles to prick us all anew. And I worry that in our hurry to leave the nineteenth century behind us, we'll turn our backs on the lessons we should have learned from the past.

Ah, maybe that's just because I'm getting old! I don't usually feel old, if truth be told, for I'm just 56. Actually, my family believes I'm 62, and in the eyes of my granddaughter, that's ancient. She means everything she says in a most loving way, but when she asks about what life was like "way back then" when I was a girl, I want to head for my rocking chair before I begin to answer. Or maybe she's right. My husband's dead, along with his mother and sisters who used to live in this house. My childhood family is a dim memory. My father died before the end of the Civil War, and my mother shortly thereafter. Even my sister Elizabeth, weakened as she was by the years she spent working in the terrible conditions of the cotton mills here in town, has been gone now for nearly twenty years.

I sometimes feel that I'm the last of a generation, hanging on to my own history by my fingernails.

There are times when I feel quite lonely, and other times when I am content to live accompanied only by Gingersnap, the big orange tomcat given to me by my daughter-in-law when my Philistine of a son would not let his young daughters keep a pet. I've always had cats. As a child the barn cats were my best friends and confidantes. Even during the war years, stray kittens found me with surprising regularity, most of them appearing when I most needed a friend or someone to cuddle. I've learned from them, too. Cats are fiercely independent, but at the same time loyal to those who love them. I've tried to imitate them in that respect. This current fellow is a good example. He has grown from a scrap of orange fur to a handsome fellow of some seventeen pounds. He chooses his friends cautiously and does not hesitate to attack with tooth and claw if someone insults his dignity. But come a quiet night like tonight and he can always be found in my lap or cuddled against my hip or shoulder. He seems to sense when I am sad or simply need his company. There are many worse fates than growing old with a faithful cat by your side.

Eh! Enough! Come on, Nellie! I'm not quite ready for the grave yet. I used to hate my mousy brown hair, but I'm grateful for it now. I always wanted sleek black hair, but the girls who took such pride in their dark locks are gray now, or white, and there's no way to hide that for long. Whereas for me, the grey hairs, coarse and wiry though they can be, blend into the lighter brown and make me almost look blonde. I've been lucky, too, with a firmness to my skin that seems to be staving off the wrinkles. At least so far, all I notice is some crinkling around the corners of my eyes, which makes it look like I'm smiling, even when I'm not. I have the usual aches and pains, and something seems to have stolen my waistline entirely. I'm not as tall as I used to be, which wasn't very tall to begin with, and sometimes I feel like my ribcage is sitting right on my hipbones. My fingers are beginning to twist a bit, and a couple of knuckles are swollen and sore. But overall, I can cut a pretty dignified figure of a woman when put to it. That's not what I worry about. I'd much rather grow old than die, and I fully expect to keep a few of my looks and my wits about me to the bitter end. I don't fear death, either. It will come when it will, and I don't expect it to be any different than falling asleep.

What I do fear is the loss of relevance—not just my own, but that of my whole generation. We lived through what was arguably the greatest of all challenges to this country and its people. The Civil War—or the War to Preserve the Union—or the War of Northern Aggression—or the War Between the States—whatever you choose to call it, it tested every one of us. Some hid from it, others denied it, or whistled it away, and some plunged headlong into it, sure they were supporting the "Right Cause," and doing the "Will of God." I've never understood the "Will of God" explanation. I don't see how anyone who knew what life on a battlefield was like could believe for a moment in a loving God who would want such events to transpire. The numbers of the dead and missing defied the imagination. The life-scarring wounds of the survivors made one wonder whether they were really lucky to have escaped death. And the heartbreaking losses of brothers, husbands, lovers, fathers, and sons scarred unknown thousands of lives. The only possible justification of such carnage might be that the war provided an admonition that it must never happen again. But not if people forget.

That's the danger I see in this excitement over the coming of the twentieth century. "Surely now we can forget the past," people seem to be saying. "Things will be different now. Things will be better. Don't keep bringing up old grievances, old stories. They are dead for us. We need to look to the future and forget the past." And my family is no better than anyone else—maybe worse.

My son Chase, for example. He's a handsome man, going a bit to flab as he matures, but handsome nevertheless. He was a bright boy from the start, and never any trouble. He sailed through school on native intelligence and followed in his father's and grandfather's footsteps to Dartmouth, law school, and the bar. He's a competent lawyer, I give him that. His problem is that he has little if any soul. He acts as society expects him to act. He is a dutiful son, a faithful husband, and a good provider for his two little girls. He pays his bills, is punctual, and obeys the laws of the land. But he doesn't care—about anything! He wants his three square meals a day, a newspaper to read, a good cigar and a jigger of whiskey in the evening, and a quiet night. That's his life. We women around him serve his basic needs and shelter him from the day-to-day irritations of life. He doesn't want to know how we feel, or what we worry about. He cares nothing about emotions or passions or fears. And so we don't tell him.

What may be worse is that he is teaching his family to turn off their emotions in the same way. Because Chase has always regarded his marriage as a matter of social convenience, his wife Mary has learned not to expect any sort of closeness within that marriage. She has a husband that she takes care of, at least in matters of seeing to it that his shirts are ironed and his meals are cooked. There's not a flicker of dust in her house, and not an iota of love, either. That might disturb the quiet perfection in which they pretend to live. Ah, but the children! Those two beautiful little girls. Mary Margaret is still too much of a baby to understand the depths of her deprivation, but my namesake Ellen, "Little Nell," knows that there is something missing in her young life. She is hungry, although she doesn't yet understand what it is that she hungers for. Thus she has become my project—my *raison d'être,* if you will.

The family has been here for Christmas. Even Chase, dullard that he usually is, seems to realize that Christmas is more about family than anything else. They live their busy, arid lives in Massachusetts, but they come home to Saco, Maine, when they need a dose of warmth and Mama's cooking. I love having them here even as I despair at the emptiness of their lives. Mainly that's because of my little Ellen, who could brighten a coal cellar with her smile and her giggles.

On Christmas night, she and I were curled up on the sofa in front of the fireplace. The Christmas goose had been picked down to the bones, the chestnut stuffing and roasted potatoes had disappeared, and Chase and Mary had taken themselves off to bed after a last cranberry cordial. But Ellen and I lingered on, lazily cracking the last walnuts from her stocking and watching the logs burn down to embers. Even the cat, Gingersnap, had finally settled down. He had had a busy day, full of ribbon chasing, goose scrap stealing, watching the snowflakes pile up on the windowsill, and batting around the occasional cranberry that fell to the floor. Now he is curled in front of the fire, tail carefully wrapped around his nose and paws to keep himself warm, dreaming of whatever a cat dreams of when his every wish has been granted.

Ellen's only ten, but she's the kind of good conversationalist who knows instinctively when to speak her mind and when to enjoy a shared silence. This was one of those silent times, when our love for each other needed no words. But eventually she giggled, and when I looked at her inquiringly, she launched a crucial discussion.

"Know what's so funny, Gran? Papa thinks you used to be a soldier. He said that when you were young, you went off to war, just like a man. He's so silly!"

I took a deep breath, giving myself a moment to think about how I wanted to respond. "Well, Nell, your Papa may not always be right, but there's usually a grain or two of truth in what he says."

"Really? You were a soldier?" She sat up straight, her eyes wide with excitement as she stared at my old face.

"Ah, not exactly. But I was an army nurse, and I did go off to war with a Union regiment during the Civil War."

Oh! How exciting! I didn't know girls were allowed to do such things. Was it wonderful?"

"Not very wonderful, I'm afraid. But yes, it was exciting at times."

"You must tell me everything about it." She cocked her head at me, caught up in a sudden burst of understanding. "So that's how you know just what to do when we get sick. You always seem to know more than the doctors."

"Don't exaggerate, dear. But yes, I have quite a little notebook of home remedies that proved successful in the field."

"In the field? Oh, you mean when you were at war! Please, tell me what it was like. Where did you go? Did you see actual fighting, and wounds, and cannon balls, and everything?" She was up on her knees now, bouncing with anticipation.

"It's a long story, Nell, and we're already up long your bedtime. But I'll tell you what. Why don't I write it down for you? You'll be headed back to Boston tomorrow, but I can send you letters, and in them I'll tell you what I remember of those days. Perhaps you can keep them all together, and some day read the whole story."

"You mean I'd have my very own book about your life, written just for me? Oh, Gran! Please, please, please do it."

And so I must begin. Can I tell this child everything that happened to me? Well, why not? If I'm going to pass on the lessons I learned during those years, she'll have to see them in context. I don't want to shelter her, the way I did with Chase. I wanted to keep him safe and protected from all the ugliness of the world. So I hid things from him. Edward and I never talked about local gossip or discussed the things we knew were wrong with the world or in our lives. I thought that if Chase grew up with only happy thoughts, he'd be a happy man. Instead, I failed to prepare him for the world in which he lives. Not only did I not teach him how to take action against injustice and evil, I failed to let him know that such things even exist. So today he moves blindly through his days, not noticing things that would make my heart break. I'll not let that happen to Nell. She's strong enough to hear about ugliness, and caring enough to want to correct it. I must show her what to look for and where to find it.

One other dilemma bothers me as I prepare to write. How do I describe to my young granddaughter the woman I was forty years ago? I scarcely recognize that woman myself. Nellie Marie Chase: a runaway 17-year-old, the discontented daughter of a dour Maine farmer and his browbeaten wife . . . a silly smidgen of a girl, too easily wooed away by a handsome young musician who played expertly on emotions she didn't even realize she had . . . a young woman forced to grow up rapidly in the smoky back rooms of gambling halls where the air reeked of alcohol, vomit, and unwashed bodies . . . a survivor learning to do whatever was necessary, no matter how degrading, in order to stay alive.

Or am I really Nellie Chase Leath: gutsy independent woman, standing up at last to a man who hit her once too often . . . daring military volunteer, offering her rather ill-defined skills to a regiment of backwoods farm boys who had no more idea than she about the conflict toward which they were headed . . . surprisingly efficient nurse, drawing on a lifetime of observations to find cures for the ill and palliatives for the terminally stricken . . . an unabashed liar who feigned a marriage vow that never happened and created for herself a history that concealed her genteel origins . . . and an expert at play-acting, living in her imagination the kind of life that had always seemed just out of her reach?

Or am I the woman my granddaughter knows: Nellie Eastman, Mrs. Edward Eastman, wife, and now widow, of a prominent Saco attorney . . . living in the stately home that she had always dreamed of having . . . spending years taking care of a rather insipid mother-in-law who had no understanding of her new daughter-in-law, and wanted none . . . watching her kind and plain-faced husband set off each morning for a brisk two-block walk to his law office on the Square with relief that he was out from under foot for the day . . . staunchly erecting barriers that would protect her small family from harm's way . . . and, in the process, firmly shutting the gates against her own feelings?

Well, if I am to put America's Civil War into its rightful place as the central event, the lynchpin, of the 19th century, I must start with the 1860 Nellie, and let the others fill in where they will. In many ways Nellie Chase Leath is the person with whom I am least familiar. She came into existence with the war and disappeared at its end. So I must let her speak for her, and perhaps I will learn as much about her as will my dear "Little Nell."

Enlistment Fears

Poor Colonel Leasure! I understand that he was trying to be helpful when he called me in and handed me the paper to sign. All I needed to do was put my name on the line and I would be a signed and sealed, certified member of the Union Army. That would mean paydays and a guarantee of a pension when I'm old and gray. Why on earth would I refuse? The poor man—I know he didn't understand.

I was really making life difficult for him, and he had more important things to do than deal with my silly hesitations. The whole camp was getting packed up to move out within hours. This was just a minor detail that needed to be wrapped up now that the Roundheads had their official designation as the 100th Pennsylvania Volunteer Infantry Regiment. So he should be forgiven for yelling at me. "Just do it, Nellie!"

But I couldn't, and I couldn't explain it to him either. I suppose I'm lucky he didn't send me home right then and there. He was puzzled, and angry, and impatient. But to give him his due, he is never unfair or unkind. So I'm still here, although I suspect I would be well advised to stay out of his way for a while. He said we'd talk about it again, when things are a bit more settled. Are things ever settled in time of war, I wonder? Never mind. At least now I have time to think about my situation here, and time to decide whether this is what I really want to do with my life.

I surely never set out to become an army nurse. When I presented myself at the Roundhead camp in Pittsburgh, I was simply looking for a place to hide. I thought it would be a temporary move, over in a few months, a way to get away from Pittsburgh and the Pointe with my virtue more or less intact. I was thinking solely of myself, despite the argument I made about being able to help the war effort.

Now he wants me to join up officially. But I'm not a joiner. I don't like being a part of a group. I didn't even like being a part of a family, where I was expected to act in accordance with some set of family customs that did not define me. I don't want to be responsible for someone else. And I don't want to become dependent on those around me. I'm a loner. And I intend to stay a loner. No more disappointments for me. No more heartbreaks. No more loneliness. And no, that's not a contradiction. A loner is not lonely. When you're lonely, it means you need someone else. When you're a loner, you've learned to need nobody. That's me, all over.

We come into this world alone, and we're pretty much left to figure things out on our own. My father, dour old farmer that he was, hoped that a new baby would mean someone to inherit his farm. He wanted a son; a daughter was only a nuisance. He spent my entire childhood ignoring me. My mother was kind enough, and she took good physical care of me, as far as she was able. But she was too harried and overworked to spare any time to develop an emotional attachment to me. Amos and

Mary Francis Chase, a good American family, attended church regularly, supported the local grange, and kept an organized and tidy farm. Mother's silver tea set was always polished. Each chair had its own set of lace doilies. Each child was spit-washed and wearing neatly mended socks. Laundry was done every Monday. Cows were milked before dawn and before sunset. Pickles and jams lined the fruit cellar shelves. But no one ever sang a lullaby or played a silly game. My sister Elizabeth and I learned early to be quiet and stay out of the way. We didn't even form a sisterly bond, because no one had ever showed us how to express affection.

Most of what I've seen of life tells me that conditions don't change that much when you grow up. People take care of themselves first. If you want to stay alive, you learn to do the same. True, most mothers take care of their children while they are little, but those ties break down when the child grows up. A mother cat will care for her kittens, too, for six or eight weeks, but then she drops them off along some country road and never looks back. If she comes face to face with them a few months later, she'll fight them as strangers.

The books I read while growing up suggested that every young woman could meet a Prince Charming and live happily ever after. Hah! Whoever wrote those stories never lived in a boarding house like the Arsenal, where all those Prince Charmings turned into sour old drunks and their suffering wives grew old before their time, often permanently scarred by the beatings they took when the money ran out. We die alone, too. Not even the best doctor in the world can prevent that. So what sense is there in trying to make permanent connections with those around us? Other people weren't with us when we arrived. They frequently make our life worse while we're here.

And they won't be with us when we check out. So what's the point?

That's the way I look at life, but I'm not sure I can explain myself to Colonel Leasure. I'm pretty sure he lives in a very different kind of world. I know he would be puzzled by my attitudes, but I have to admit that it would bother me if he disapproved of them. I don't need him—or his regiment—but my life is more pleasant if those around me consider themselves my friends. I want to be liked. I am willing to like those around me in return. But I don't want to be bound to them. I don't want to be responsible for them. I don't want to measure my self-worth by their standards. I just want to be me, doing what I can as well as I can, without needing anyone else.

So, no, Colonel Leasure. I will not sign your papers. I'll travel with the regiment so long as I feel I can be of use. I'll do my job efficiently and dispassionately. And when the time comes, I'll move on with no regrets and no broken relationships. That will have to be enough for you and for the Army. It's the only way I know to keep myself whole.

Hurricanes

Memories are physical. I don't think I ever fully realized that until I tried to recall how I felt during the hurricane of 1861. And I'm not talking here about the physical sensations of rough seas, lashing winds, and driving rain. Rather, I'm remembering and experiencing the gut-wrenching pain and hollowness of those hours after the storm, when I had to face and identify my fears. A hollow feeling pervaded my being. My mouth felt as if it had no upper palate—that the roof of my mouth went clear to the top of my skull. My head was just a hollow balloon, ready to pop at any moment. My stomach was the same way. I was just a shell—no substance, no mass, and no beating heart—just emptiness.

I was nobody. I'd often suspected that, of course, but lying there in sickbay, strapped to a narrow bunk, I lost my identity entirely. Oh, I knew who I was pretending to be. I told people I was twenty-four years old, separated by the war from my musician husband, who had gone off to join a regimental band in Ohio. My name was Mrs. Leath, and I served at my own pleasure as Matron of the Roundhead Regiment. But if someone from the Army had gone off to find out more about me, he would have found no trace of that person. My name was not Leath, nor had it ever been. I was barely eighteen, a runaway probably sought by the law, the doxy of a man who had been a gambler, a liar, a forger, and a thief. I knew nothing of the healing arts I tried to practice, and the remedies I offered were not ones I had learned at the knee of my wise old grandmother. They were simply tidbits I had gleaned from fillers in the news-papers, when I was looking for some way to fool the Army into accepting me as a nurse.

In short, I had constructed a cloak of lies under which I could conceal my true identity. The lies had multiplied, as lies must always do in order to avoid detection, until they formed a tightly woven fabric that enfolded and smothered me.

I had once been the daughter of a prosperous farming fam-ily in Saco, Maine. I was raised in genteel fashion to take my rightful, though modest, place in society. My parents meant for me to find an acceptable young man, a younger son whose own family position would encourage him to marry into our family and take over from my father as proprietor of Pinecrest Farm. That was my responsibility, since my older sister Elizabeth, with her plain face, protruding teeth, fragile health, and hang-dog attitude seemed likely to be headed for spinsterhood.

Almost no one had ever asked what I wanted out of life. And my rebellious seventeen-year-old self resented that failure. The head mistress at my school, however, had suggested that I was bright and would make a good teacher. If I went off to Normal School after graduation, she promised, she would hire me to come back and teach classes in her school. Normal School had sounded positively exotic to a girl who had never been off the farm, and I was cockily sure of myself when I told my father that was what I wanted to do. He laughed at me.

That laughter set me on a disastrous path. I took my first opportunity to escape the family I thought was thwarting my deepest desires. A traveling musician lured me away with his deep blue eyes, his curly black hair, and a silver tongue to match his golden horn. I ran away with him and began to weave the fabric of lies that eventually enveloped and destroyed every trace of that innocent young girl.

So there I was. I had lost the person I had been, and the person I had become was a fraud. That's where the tears came from—the tears I could not control for hours after my accident. I cried not because I was injured. How can you injure someone who doesn't exist? I wasn't afraid of death. Death would have been a welcome release from a life of deception. I wasn't trying to get pity from my companions. I knew I did not deserve pity. I was in mourning for the life I had lost. And I mourned for the lost confidence that had once allowed me to look forward to the future. I lay on that cot and saw nothing but a blackness ahead of me—no hopes, no better days to come, no purpose in life, no filling up of this emptiness that pervaded my body—and my soul. People passed by me—whole people, people who had lives to live and jobs to do, people who mattered, people full of potential. I was no longer one of them. Doctor Ludington had said he wanted me to rest. That was easy now. I simply could not muster the energy to move.

How long might I have lain there, sunk into my very own slough of despond? I didn't care. I just wanted to be left alone to adjust to my nothingness. But remaining alone was next to impossible on a ship crowded with over 1500 people. During the second long night, when the hurricane had blown itself out and the seas had calmed, I became aware of a figure standing next to my cot. A young soldier had come to sickbay seeking a sticking plaster for a minor cut. While there, he asked after me, and Doctor Ludington had pointed to where I lay.

"Scuse, ma'am. I didn't mean to wake you. I jus' wanted to make sure you were all right."

"I'm fine," I mumbled.

"We've all been right worried about you, ma'am. I was there. I mean, I saw you fall, and I was that scared for you."

"Do I know you?" I asked, wondering why he was there at all.

"Prob'ly not. My name's Jim McCaskey, from Company C. Some of my friends have had dealings with you. You taught a couple of them to play poker. But me? No, I'm just one of the boys. We all know you, though, and we'd be in deep trouble if we'd lost you. "

"I doubt that."

"You're important to us, ma'am. You remind me of home and of my sister, Sarah Jane. She's older'n me by a couple of years, and I always knew I could go to her if I needed somebody to talk to. You seem like the same sort. Not that I need somebody to talk to right now, but it gives me comfort to know you're here if I do. So I jus' wanted to make sure you'd be back, cheering us all up and keeping us lively."

He went on his way, and I discovered that my head was feeling a bit more normal. I pulled the blankets closer around me, still not ready to venture beyond my cot, and began to reconsider my options. What could I do with the revelations that had come to me with the accident?

I had faced the fact that I was living a lie. Could I correct that? Could I go to Colonel Leasure and tell him that I was on the run from the law and a cluster of unpaid debts? That I had joined the regiment not out of patriotism but out of desperation? Could I go to Doctor Ludington and confess the source of my herbal knowledge? Could I tell the other nurses that I was not like them—not a wife separated from a beloved husband or a mother separated from her son by the war, but little more than a loose woman, betrayed by a scoundrel? Could I go to Reverend Browne and confess that he was right about me? Could I offer to leave? To resign and go back to Pittsburgh?

That thought, at least, brought a small smile to my face. I was on a ship in the middle of the Atlantic, and there would be no leaving here before landfall, unless I were prepared to throw myself overboard. A day earlier I might have done just that, but young McCaskey's words echoed in my empty head. Somebody, at least, needed me to stay put. So could I admit my lies and still remain where I was? Unlikely! Besides, what good would it do? I might alleviate my own guilt, but the rest of the folks on board would not be better off because of my revelations.

Obviously, there was no way I could ago back to being little Nellie Chase after being Mrs. Leath. Little Nellie didn't exist anymore, nor did the world in which she lived. There was no going back. My only choice was to go forward as Nellie Chase Leath, re-creating her as I went along. And then, for some reason, I remembered the words of poor, dying Billy Sample one long night en route to Annapolis: "When this here war's over, I'm gonna try to be the kind of man my dog Charlie thinks I am." I had seen that as a commendable goal, not as a way to hide his own identity.

Perhaps I could redefine myself the way Billy had intended to. I couldn't go backward, but I could go forward, trying to become the kind of woman the boys of the Roundhead

Regiment thought I was. And so I did. I gingerly crawled out of the cocoon I had made of my blankets, found my dampish dress, and went out to see what conditions were like on deck.

Spring Interlude

When I look back now, it's hard to remember what happened during the spring of 1862. It was a chaotic time, filled with more emotion than reasoned decision-making. For myself, I had reached a point at which I was content and no longer poised to run away at the first sign of trouble. But I had not yet found a real purpose for my life, a destination to run to, if you will. My personal life was simply on hold, and a great relief it was. For the soldiers stationed in the Sea Islands, however, there was much distress.

I do remember the weather and how miserable it was. We had all become used to the idea that January and February felt like spring. We had basked in the warm sun, smelled the intoxicating fragrances of camellias and magnolias and had laughed over stories from home about slush and grime. Then, without much warning, we hit the rainy season. It rained for days on end, never really a hard downpour but a constant, steady drizzle. Soon the fine sandy soil of South Carolina had reached its saturation point, and everything turned to that sticky mess called pluff mud. Vegetation decayed in the mud, small creatures died in it, and it smelled like rotten eggs. The poor soldiers who were still living in tents suffered the most. The dampness permeated everything, and the mud coated their boots and their belongings.

As a result, disease began to spread through the camps. Many of the men suffered from colds, and a troubling percentage developed pneumonia. We had new epidemics of measles, typhoid, malaria, and dysentery. There were even a few cases of mumps. Robert Moffatt was laid low by the swellings in his jaw and spent ten days in the regimental hospital. He tried not to grumble, but when it snowed one day in March while he was confined to his bed, he argued mightily to be allowed to go out and at least throw a snowball or two. We didn't let him, of course, and the men who were living in the damp cold were not sympathetic. For them, the cold weather was simply another insult aimed at making their lives more miserable. The medical staff was suffering, too, from overwork and crowded conditions. We had beds lined up in the hallways, and some patients who were recovering from wounds of various sorts found they had been assigned to thin pads on the floor.

The war news was another great source of discontent. Daily dispatches were reporting heavy fighting in several areas. Union victories at Fort Donelson and at Shiloh changed the course of the war in Tennessee. The Mississippi River and its great port of New Orleans fell into Union control. It was all good news, but we had not shared in it. It seemed to the men of the South Carolina Expeditionary Force that they had been forgotten. They sat in the midst of pluff mud and swamp, guarding empty islands from non-existent Confederate troops. There was no glory to the war from what they could see. Except for that one contrived little skirmish on New Year's Day, most of them had never fired a shot nor heard one fired at them. The war began to seem like a waste of time, and the men themselves felt useless.

There was, to be sure, one Northern victory during those months, as the Navy and a small battery of new rifled cannons managed to take out Fort Pulaski, which protected the city of Savannah, Georgia, south of us. It was a promising start, but it, too, petered out as the Army high command refused to follow up the victory. As for my poor little Roundheads, they missed even that small victory. Two days before the scheduled attack, the 100th Pennsylvania was ordered to march out in the opposite direction from Fort Pulaski. So out they went, camped for a couple of days, and then traipsed back after the initial excitement over the victory had died down. They had provided a distraction, I suppose, in case any Confederate spies were watching to see what was going on in our camps. But for these recruits who had been champing at the bit to see a bit of action, it was just one more time when they had been pushed aside as other troops engaged the enemy.

The worst blow to morale was a change of command. General Thomas W. Sherman had been in charge of our expedition from its very beginnings, and the regiments he had recruited to accompany him were intensely loyal to him. He had been locked in a protracted struggle with Admiral DuPont over the respective duties of the Army and the Navy. It was true that some people blamed him for the failure of the Army to pursue a more aggressive course in South Carolina. Still, it came as a shock when he was abruptly recalled and replaced by the more decisive General David Hunter. To complicate matters even further, General Hunter immediately placed one of his younger cronies, General Henry Washington Benham, in charge of all military operations. Suddenly no one from brigade commanders on down knew what to expect. All their careful reconnaissance efforts and projected plans to capture the city of Charleston were simply ignored. If the enlisted men had been disaffected before, their officers now joined them.

I can't speak of Benham's and Hunter's military skills because I don't understand enough about such things. But I did see General Hunter make one terrible blunder that effectively destroyed everything that had been accomplished in regard to the slaves. Several officers had tried to explain to him the problems created by having the islands inhabited by large numbers of slaves whose masters had abandoned them. Finally Hunter threw up his hands. "Their masters are gone? Nobody owns them? We certainly don't own them. They are free."

"But, sir," one colonel ventured. "It just doesn't work like that. They don't have citizenship. Their status is still that of slaves, and President Lincoln has not issued any orders about freeing the slaves."

"So I'll do it." He scribbled a few words on a handy sheet of paper. He first declared martial law, and then ended with this statement: "The persons in these three States, Georgia, Florida, and South Carolina, heretofore held as slaves, are therefore declared forever free." The proclamation was patently illegal, but there it was. And Hunter immediately followed it with an even more damaging move. Just two days later, he announced that he was forming a colored regiment manned by the former slaves because they were now free citizens of the United States. The move was to be implemented by young staff officers. These poor young men were sent out to each plantation to announce that all able-bodied men between the ages of eighteen and forty-five were to be transported immediately to Hilton Head to be sworn into the army.

General Stevens' son, Captain Hazard Stevens, was one of those who delivered the bad news. He later described the scene as the men were called from the fields and loaded into transport wagons. They were given no explanations, no time to gather coats or shoes, no time to say farewell to their families. Hazard said the weeping of wives and the wailing of children haunted him for weeks.

The move did not last, of course. President Lincoln erupted in fury over this attempt to take over his authority. He immediately issued his own proclamation, declaring that any such emancipation decree purporting to free the slaves before he had made his own determination was "altogether void." The slaves who had been so unceremoniously carted off came home within ten days, and there was no more official talk about freedom. But the effects were long ranging.

Most of the slaves—at least the ones I knew—understood nothing about the emancipation decree or about its repeal. Uncle Bob, however, had heard the details, and understood fully what it might mean to him. As soon as Hunter's proclamation had become known, I had overheard Uncle Bob talking to our housemaid, Maybelle. "From now on, Miss Maybelle, you may call me Mr. Hankins." I found it a poignant moment, and without being told, I tried to remember to use that form of address when I spoke to our household manager. "Mr. Hankins" fairly beamed with pride at that small nod to his dignity, even though the decree itself did not last long.

Others were not so happy. The cotton agents were infuriated that the soldiers had come in and disrupted their planting. Even after the slaves returned to work, the agents complained that the slaves were now too independent. They would slip off for a day or two and then come back nonchalantly to resume their duties, thus throwing off all the carefully laid out plans of the agents who were trying to teach them proper agricultural practices. The missionaries, too, were upset. They were still trying to get their schools organized. One argument they used to encourage people to come was that education would prepare them for citizenship. That appeal weakened when citizenship had been offered without any such requirement.

All in all, the months of March, April, and May were miserable ones. Life's little inconveniences loomed large when people were already unhappy. Complaints engendered more complaints. Spirits were low, and hopes had been dashed. We desperately needed a change. Whether the change we got was worth it had yet to be determined.

August Interlude

In August I was fired. Rumors aboard the ship that was carrying the Roundheads to a new campaign in Virginia swirled around my head and led to Colonel Leasure's announcement that I would be dismissed as soon as we reached land. I don't remember much about the rest of the voyage. I might have been able to accept the firing without falling apart. But when Colonel Leasure suggested that my actions might have compromised his own future ability to lead his men into battle, I was devastated. I could not even begin to accept the idea that men might die of horrible battle wounds because of something I had done. A small part of me argued that he was exaggerating. My sin was too small to have such widespread results. I had only smuggled a tiny kitten on board the ship. But then came the other voices, led by that of Reverend Browne, all of them saying, "You're the sinner. Their blood is on your hands."

I crawled into my berth and lay there shivering for a long time. Days? Perhaps. Gradually I became aware of a piercing pain in my right side. It felt like a sharp dagger was being inserted between my ribs. When I tried to stand, I could only mange to stay erect at all by clutching that side and bending over. I was feverish, too, I suspected, but I could not bring myself to call for help. I just pulled the covers up tighter around my chin and hoped that I was going to die there. Food arrived on schedule and the guard would bring it in, but I always pretended to be asleep. Once in a while I tried to manage a few bites, but everything tasted like sawdust. The guard made no comment when he took the untouched meals away.

I knew they would be saying that Nellie was just being melodramatic again, but I didn't really care what anyone thought. I could not bear to think of the same people who had condemned me offering false sympathy if I did indeed prove to be ill. I simply waited for time to pass. I could not think about the future, because I could not imagine how horrible it would be. They were sending me back to Pittsburgh, that filthy, evil city I had worked so hard to escape. The boarding house loomed, more offers of prostitution, more gossipy folks ready to carry the word of my return to Otis Leath. Fear and revulsion fought for top place on my list of emotions.

When we docked in Newport News, the colonel sent Sergeant Stevens to be sure I was ready to depart. He found me still lying in my berth, unable to make myself move.

"Nellie, are you ill?"

"I don't know."

"Can you stand up?"

"I suppose so." But when I tried to stand, the pain in my side was so severe that I had to grasp the side of the berth to keep from falling over. I clutched it while sweat beaded on my forehead.

"I'm going to get Colonel Leasure," he said in a panic.

"No," I managed to gasp. "Get Doctor Ludington." While he was gone, I lowered myself gingerly into a sitting position, and it was there that the kindly doctor found me.

"My God," I heard him gasp. "Nellie, how long have you been like this? You look ghastly."

I simply shook my head. "I don't know," I told him. "Ever since the colonel locked me in here," I wanted to say, but the room started to spin and go dark.

The next thing I remember was waking up on a cot in a military tent. Mary Pollock was there with me, waiting to take orders from the doctors who stood around me.

"It seems like appendicitis," one young medical student suggested. "But the pain is on the wrong side."

"Her temperature is not all that elevated. I think she has just fretted and stewed herself into this state. The guard reports that she hasn't eaten in three days. That alone could cause her to faint and suffer cramps."

"I don't think so," I heard Doctor Ludington argue. "Mary, get her undressed and into this overlarge gown. I'm going to want to see that portion of her side where she keeps touching and then wincing."

Mary must have had quite a struggle getting my clothes removed, because I was unable to be of any help. All I could do was cry out whenever she touched me too firmly. But at last the task was finished. The staff officers returned, and with a great show of preserving my modesty, they gradually managed to uncover a portion of my right ribcage below the breast. There was a collective intake of breath.

"What is that?" someone asked.

I wanted to ask the same question, but I was too far out of it to formulate the words . . . or to understand what I heard them saying next: "inflammation, pustules, oozing liquid, scabs forming in layers, like shingles."

In my confused state of consciousness, I remember thinking, "They've mistaken me for a roof!" Or did I say it out loud? I'm not really sure. Then they rolled me onto my side and uncovered my back.

"See how the lesions cover her whole right side while the left side remains unaffected? She definitely has a bad case of shingles."

If I hadn't hurt so badly, I might have giggled. Instead, I passed out again. I regained consciousness once or twice, each time hearing disembodied voices discussing my condition as if I were not even in the room.

"She's too young to have shingles."

"Not if she had recently had a terrifying experience."

"I still think she's faking it."

"What can be done for her?"

"Nothing. Shingles is not a fatal disease; it just makes you wish you were dead."

"We can't leave her in this condition."

"No, but we can't take her with us, either. She's not fit to travel, even if General Stevens would allow it, which he won't."

"Keep giving her morphine—enough to keep her under without killing her—while we find a place to put her."

Then someone was lifting me onto a litter, and two men carried me out of the tent. They had trouble holding the litter steady, and the jostling movement sent such searing pain through my side that I passed out again.

I realize now that part of the problem was that I had never before been really ill. I didn't know how to feel so ill that I could surrender myself to the care of others and accept them as they tried to help me. Instead, I was fighting their efforts whenever I was conscious enough to do so. I was frightened, angry, and so overcome with despair that I would have willingly died at any moment. At times, I actually prayed to die. I'm happy I didn't, however. Look at all I would have missed.

A Voice from the Past

Nellie was not particularly happy with the decision to send her to Baltimore to accompany the wounded soldiers from Fredericksburg. She was tempted to argue with the Army officers who were casually assigning medical personnel without regard for their preferences. Luckily, however, she remembered that her disobedience had once resulted in dismissal from the Roundhead Regiment. The pain of that memory was enough to dissuade her from complaint.

Nevertheless, her memory of the Roundheads traversing the city in the middle of the night to avoid being attacked by a pro-southern mob was still vivid. If she had been asked to describe that city, she would have pictured ramshackle huts, filthy streets, and bands of thugs waiting to attack the unwary. In 1863, Maryland was still very much a border state. Although Maryland had not seceded, a majority of its citizens were opposed to Lincoln's presidency and ready to fight over their right to hold slaves. The president had placed Baltimore under martial law to help protect the troops who passed through its rail terminals each day, but dangers still threatened. There had even been talk of an assassination plot when Lincoln passed through the city.

Balancing that impression of the city as a whole were the favorable reports of the hospital to which most of the Fredericksburg survivors were assigned. Major General George H. Steuart, CSA, had owned a mansion with nearly four acres of grounds at the western edge of the city. It stood on high ground, overlooking the city and its harbor. When the Steuarts threw their support to the Confederacy in 1861, the U. S. Government had confiscated the estate to serve as a military hospital. They had erected enough barracks to house some 1500 patients, while still preserving much of the beauty of the estate. The barracks themselves surrounded the formal estate gardens, which provided a peaceful and invigorating exercise area for those men who were ambulatory. The air was fresh, the accommodations clean and well furnished, and the rations plentiful. The women of Baltimore worked tirelessly as volunteers, providing assistance to the staff of nine doctors and 130 nurses.

It was the best possible destination for Nellie's patients, and she reluctantly agreed to accompany them. Clean sheets, nourishing meals, comfortable mattresses, and smiling faces went a long way to keep the patients happy. And when they were content in their surroundings, their recovery periods were shorter.

One of her patients was so grateful for the care he had received in Baltimore that he decided to fall in love with his nurse. When he proposed marriage to Nellie, she told another lie. "I'm sorry. I'm married. I thought you knew that."

What Nellie couldn't tell him—or anyone, for that matter—was that she felt incapable of loving anyone. It wasn't just that her heart had been broken when she discovered the truth about Otis Leath. It was also hearing the accusations made by Reverend Browne. When he condemned her for her relationship with Daniel Leasure, he was actually suggesting that being in love was sinful. In her rational moments, Nellie didn't believe that, but she kept hearing the accusations over and over in her head. They made her feel guilt about a love she hadn't ever felt.

~~~

When she was really truthful with herself, she began to question whether she had ever experienced love. Certainly her feelings for Otis Leath could have been explained away by simple infatuation. And as for family love, well, she had no idea what that was. There hadn't been any love in her family, at least none she had seen. Her father was cold and vicious most of the time. Her mother was a mousy little creature who took care of her family out of a sense of duty, not love. Nellie could not remember her mother showing affection to her two daughters, either. She kept them clean and well fed, but she never hugged them spontaneously or told them how much they meant to her.

So there I am, she lectured herself. Some kind of flawed person—one who can't make a connection to anyone else. My infatuation with Otis turned to scorn and then to disgust and fear. I respected Colonel Leasure, but when he fired me I was able to walk away and never tried to correct his erroneous impressions. Several of my patients have been fine, upstanding young men, and I know, deep down, that some of them think they have fallen in love with me, but I can feel nothing in return. My only real experience of love has been what I have felt for my cats. And what kind of pathetic creature admits that?

Nellie's way of dealing with her feelings, or lack of them, was to throw herself into her work. Nursing was one way she could reach out to another human being. She could demonstrate that she cared by the simple expedient of a cool hand against a fevered brow, or by a word of encouragement to someone who was feeling down. She was there with a cheerful smile to celebrate each small triumph. She made an extra cup of tea for a patient in need of comfort. She listened to endless stories of family and friends back home, always suggesting by her interest and enthusiasm that the patient would be going home soon. She let sunshine and fresh air into the wards whenever possible, and encouraged the ambulatory patients to join her in walks around the gardens.

No surprisingly, her wards saw a great deal of turnover, as patients developed the confidence to help with their own recoveries. Nellie inaugurated a small ritual farewell party for each man who was headed home, and those who were still there discovered in its customs a renewed hope for their own farewells. Nellie herself was content, most of the time. She took real pleasure in her successes, while trying not to think too far ahead. The end of the war might mean the end of her career, but for the time being, she was where she needed to be, and that was enough.

The restful interlude into which she had settled was interrupted in a way she might never have expected. It was an ordinary day, and she was sitting quietly at her makeshift desk, trying to get caught up on her record keeping. The young man who approached her was just an ordinary young man, too, or so she thought.

"Excuse me, Miss. I'm looking for the ward where soldiers from Maine are housed."

Nellie looked up, noticing for the first time that the gentleman leaned heavily on a cane. "Are you signing in?" she asked.

"We weren't told to expect anyone new, but I'm sure your paperwork will be along shortly."

"No, thank God," the man chuckled. "I think I'm finished with being a patient. But I should have introduced myself. I'm Captain Eastman, 6th Regiment, Maine Infantry, Army of the Potomac. Or at least I was until a minnie ball took out most of my calf muscle during the Siege of Yorktown." He gave a brief nod at his cane. "Now I've been given an honorable discharge, despite my arguments that I could still be of service, even if my stride is a little off kilter. So now I'm a lawyer again, working in my father's law office and using every excuse I can find to get out from behind my desk. Whenever I can, I do the business traveling my father no longer likes to do. And when it brings me to a city where there is an Army hospital, I use the opportunity to check up on my old comrades."

"I see," Nellie responded, smiling at his breathless explanation. "Is there someone in particular that you're looking for?"

"No. I'm actually hoping NOT to find anybody I know, but the odds of that happening are pretty low, especially after what I've heard of the Battle of Fredericksburg."

"There are men from several New England regiments here," Nellie said. "Come, I'll walk you down that way and show you the ward you want."

When they reached Ward IV, Capt. Eastman paused to look through the doorway. Suddenly the shout went up. "Hey! Look who's here!"

"Captain Eastman? What are you doing here, sir?"

"Jake, come over here. Captain Eastman's here."

"How are you?"

"Good to see you."

Nellie grinned. "I think you've found the people you were looking for," she said. She gestured for him to enter the ward. "Take your time. The men have plenty of time to visit, and we'll be happy to have you stay for lunch."

She stood for a few more minutes, watching the happy reunion. Suddenly, one comment separated itself from the general bedlam, one that made her catch her breath.

"Hey, Eddie! We heard you was back in Saco, working for your dad. That so?"

Feeling a rising fear in her chest, Nellie backed away from the door. *Back in Saco? Who is that man? Eastman? A lawyer? Eddie? Eddie Eastman?* And then she knew who he was. Her father had visited a lawyer in Saco, a man by the name of Philip Eastman. And Eastman had a son named Edward, a boy just a few years older than Nellie. She had never really met them, but most folks knew who the Eastmans were. They were a prominent family, with a fine house on Main Street, and the family law office right on the town square.

What if he's looking for me? Oh, that's silly! Unless— unless Father asked his lawyer to track me down. But he seems sincere enough about finding his old comrades. Nellie dithered. *Maybe I should just introduce myself. But what if he's not looking for me at all? That would sound awfully weird. Maybe I could just leave. I could be gone when he comes back this way, but that would be running away, and I promised myself I wouldn't do that again.*

She was still dithering when Captain Eastman came back down the hall. "Excuse me again, Miss . . . I'm afraid I didn't catch your name."

"It's Chase. Nellie Chase." There was no sense hiding her identity. It was right there on the tag on her collar.

"Well, Nurse Chase. I've spent a very pleasant morning visiting many old friends. Is it all right if I return the next time I'm in Baltimore?"

"Of course. Do you come here often?"

'Right now, we're trying to settle an inheritance case in the courts here, so, yes, I'm here a couple of times a month. I enjoy the trips. It's certainly a much livelier town than little Saco, Maine, where I come from."

Nellie tried to control her impulses, but she winced, and he noticed.

"What did I say?" he asked. "Are you familiar with Saco?"

"I . . . uh . . . I lived there once."

"Really? When was that?"

"Oh, several years ago . . . before the war."

Too late, she realized that this was another conversation she should not be having. Shut up, Nellie, she scolded herself.

"And we've never met? That's odd. I thought I knew all the pretty girls."

Nellie opened her mouth but now no words came out. He was a hopeless flatterer, but a charmer. Under normal circumstances, she might have been tempted to flirt with him a bit, but now she just wanted him gone. Unfortunately, that was not what he wanted. His curiosity was aroused, and he was determined to find out more about her.

"You said your name was Chase? There was a family by that name . . . Wait, I remember now. They had a young daughter who disappeared. The father suspected she had run off with a traveling salesman or something. And her name was . . . Nellie, too, I think. Are you that Nellie Chase?"

She felt herself flushing. "Please, just leave me alone. Don't tell my father you found me."

"Oh, dear. I think we had better talk. Is there somewhere private that we could use?"

"No! I shouldn't leave my post. A patient might need me. And I don't want to hear whatever it is you are going to say."

"No, I don't suppose you would. But apparently you don't know. Miss Chase, if you are really the daughter of Amos Chase, I have to tell you that your father is dead."

"He can't be dead. He was never sick. And he's not that old . . ." She paled, shaking her head and backing away from the bearer of bad news.

"I'm sorry. He had a stroke; it was very sudden. He was out in the fields. He didn't come in for lunch, and his wife went looking for him. Found him just lying there."

"When was this?" She wanted to know, and yet she didn't.

"Let me think. It was before I signed up, so sometime before the war broke out."

"What about my mother? Is she all right?"

"As I remember, she and your sister . . . You do have a sister, don't you?"

"Elizabeth. Yes."

"They couldn't run the farm by themselves. Our law office handled the sale. I think they moved to Boston after that. I can't be sure, but I can find out."

"No. Please, no. I don't want to know any more. Please, just leave me alone. Forget you ever met me." She turned and walked away quickly, taking refuge in the only shelter she knew, the care of her patients.

Courtship

Edward Eastman did leave, but he couldn't forget. The lovely face haunted him—so caring and gentle with her patients, so defiantly angry when he probed her background, so crumpled and devastated when she learned of her family's dissolution. He hadn't been looking for her. In fact, he probably had never thought of her since he heard the initial gossip around the time she disappeared. But now, here she was, and somehow she had become his responsibility. He prowled through the old records in his father's office, searching for clues as to what had happened to the family. He found little except the settlement of Amos Chase's estate, showing a heavily negative balance. It was accompanied by the deed of transfer, in which the family farm had been sold to pay off those debts.

"Father, do you remember the Chase family?" he asked casually.

"Chase? Amos Chase, you mean? Why would you be interested in him? He's long dead, and his bill still unpaid. But we'll never recover that. They're all gone now." His father grumbled and turned away, considering his words the final closing argument, as he did whenever an unpleasant subject arose. This time, Edward was grateful. He had no intention of explaining his interest.

Next, he turned to an old college chum who now practiced law in Cambridge. Being as circumspect as possible, he wrote to ask him to see if he could locate a woman named Mary Frances Chase and her daughter Elizabeth, originally from Saco but now thought to be living in Boston. The answer soon came back. No one with those names could be identified. There were several Elizabeth Chases and even more Mary Chases, but none that seemed to fit the ages Edward had supplied from his father's records. If they had ever been in Boston, they had left no trace.

"I should at least tell Nellie that," he thought to himself. "It won't make her feel better to know they have disappeared, but it may relieve her fear that they will suddenly turn up." And with that rationalization, he looked for an excuse to return to Baltimore.

One soon supplied itself. The inheritance case he had been working on developed a new twist, one that threw all previous dealings into question. The deceased was a prominent businessman who had had his finger in several textile companies. And, as it turned out, he had had several families, too. His second wife, who lived in Saco, was claiming a major portion of her late husband's estate for her own support and that of their two young children. There was a previous family living in Baltimore, and that first wife, still bitter over her divorce, argued that her own two grown sons were their father's legal heirs. And now came the revelations of a mistress, also from Baltimore, who claimed to have a letter in which her lover had promised to recognize her bastard son as his legal heir.

"How could this fellow not have had the sense to make a will?" Edward demanded in exasperation.

"Ah, he's exactly the type who wouldn't make a will," his father explained. "First of all, he thought he was immortal because he was wealthy. And second, his marital arrangements were so complicated that he would never have wanted to put them in writing. You don't keep secrets by revealing everything to your lawyer, no matter how trusted he may be. It's a wonderful case for you to cut your teeth on, son. It'll give you practice in arguing your client's case in front of a judge. And if you are really good, you may bring into the firm some welcome income. This fellow probably has enough wealth to support all those children . . . and us, too. I want you to spend all of your time on this case. See to it that we get our share."

Edward tried not to show his eagerness to do just that. "But, Father, it's a long trip from here to Baltimore, and this case is likely to be in and out of the courts for months. It's going to be quite costly for us to pursue our lady's claims there."

"Then maybe you ought to stay in Baltimore for a while. Take a room in a boarding house and let the warring ladies know that you intend to be there for any shenanigans they may try to pull."

"I could do that, I suppose. I'll at least look around when I'm there next week . . . see what I can find." Nodding his agreement, he went back to his desk. "And I'll sleep on a park bench if I have to," he murmured to himself.

⸺✕⸺

His first stop when he returned to Baltimore was neither the courts nor the rental agency. He headed straight for Steuart Hospital. Nellie heard the tapping of his cane before he came into sight, and her heart was already beating fast when he approached her desk, where she was studiously writing in her logbook.

"Miss Chase?"

"Oh, Captain Eastman." She glanced up with what she hoped as a startled look on her face. "What a nice surprise for your comrades. They'll be happy to see you again. You remember where the ward is located, don't you?" She hoped her message was clear. She made no comment about her own unreasonable delight to see him.

"Yes, I do remember. But first, how are you? I've been worried about you."

"Worried about me? Whatever for?"

"I delivered some bad news, and you were totally unprepared to hear it. I knew you were quite upset when I left, and I've felt guilty for disrupting your life."

"So here you are again? Bringing me some other delightful news flash from my past?"

"I have not been able to locate your mother and sister, if that's what you mean."

"I asked you not to try," she said.

"Miss Chase, please don't be angry with me for caring about you. I considered it my professional responsibility to do what I could for the daughter of a former client."

"Fine. You tried. Now can we put an end to it?"

"Certainly, if that is your wish. But I hope we don't have to put an end to a budding friendship as well."

"I didn't realize we had a budding relationship of any kind, Captain Eastman."

"I'm working at it," he confessed. "I'm going to be living in Baltimore for the next few months, and you are the only person from home that I know here. Could we just start over and be old acquaintances?"

"You didn't remember me, and I didn't remember you. That hardly qualifies as 'old acquaintances.'"

"But I'm sure we knew some of the same people . . . attended the same entertainments . . . visited the same shops. Could we give ourselves time to identify some of those connections?"

"I . . . I don't know." A war raged in Nellie's head and heart. One part of her was terrified of letting this man get to know her. The other wanted just that.

"Please. Have dinner with me tonight. I'm staying at the Railroad Hotel at Bolton Station until I can find a boarding house. They appear to have an elegant dining room, but I'd feel awkward eating there all by myself."

"Oh! I couldn't. I stay here at the hospital and take my meals in the kitchen. That way I'm always available if someone needs me. I can't just leave for the evening."

"You make this job sound like a prison sentence. It's all the more reason why you should let me take you out. You need to get away once in a while."

"But, what would everyone think?" Nellie was grasping at straws.

"I assure you, my intentions are quite honorable."

"I didn't think you were trying to . . . uh. . ."

"We'll have a lovely dinner, and I'll escort you back here before it's time for 'lights out'. No more excuses. I'll be waiting when you get off duty. . . At six, is it?"

They did indeed have a lovely dinner. Edward wisely kept the conversation light, not stressing their Saco origins but exploring Nellie's likes and dislikes. "Are you a dog person or a cat person?" he asked at one point.

"Oh, cats, definitely! It's hard to have a pet at all when you work for a military hospital, but once in a while, a stray kitten comes my way, and I can never resist."

"Why would you prefer a cat over a dog?" he challenged playfully. "Dogs obey your commands, they are loyal, they'll follow you anywhere. Cats ignore you."

"Cats are loyal and obedient, too, but you have to earn their trust. They don't just blindly leap up and lick the face of anyone who pats them on their head."

"Rather like yourself," he teased. "I keep having the feeling that I'm on some sort of probation here. How does one go about earning a cat's trust?"

"By not being too forward. By letting the cat come to you. By respecting her wishes. By trying to understand her language."

"Oh, come on," he said, laughing. "Cats meow. They don't have a language."

"Oh, but they do, once you get to know them. A cat that trusts you will ask for attention by making this strange sound in the back of her throat. It's sort of like a purr, but vocalized. And it means, 'I like you and I trust you enough to tell you what I need.' They greet you in the morning with a cute little chirp, and sometimes you can carry on a long conversation with a cat who is making little understanding comments." Nellie laughed at herself. "You must think I have quite an imagination."

"I think you've had some very lucky cats."

Nellie looked pensive for a moment, and then shook her head decisively. "I've vowed not to fall in love with another cat until I can be sure that I can spend the rest of its life taking care of it."

"That day will come," he said, hoping he was right.

Friends at Last

As the weeks passed, Nellie and Edward developed a close friendship. He was spending long hours in the courtroom, and she frequently had difficult nursing cases that required her full attention. But when both were free, they enjoyed sharing a meal, attending an occasional concert, or going for a long walk in the nearby park. Neither one of them ever spoke of love, and there was almost no physical contact between them, except when Edward took her elbow to help her up a difficult step or she brushed the crumbs from his vest. They were simply friends. Nellie found she could tell Edward anything without fear that he would judge her.

Bit by bit she revealed the details of her past—her desire to become a teacher, her elopement with the handsome horn player, the difficult days when he lost heavily at gambling and took out his frustrations on her face. She explained how she had come to join the Roundhead Regiment, and how the chaplain suspected her of being an actress or a prostitute. She told him of the terrible mistake she had made by smuggling her cat aboard the ship, her firing, and the subsequent illness that landed her in a convent. Whatever she found the courage to tell him he accepted with understanding and compassion.

He even offered to investigate the legal status of her marriage to Otis Leath. "You'll continue to consider yourself bound to him so long as you do not know whether or not you ever had a valid marriage."

"But I've told you. I don't know who the man was who married us. And I don't know whether there was ever a record of the marriage. Or whether Otis has ever divorced me."

"That's why you're lucky you have a friend in the lawyer business. It won't take long to find out where you stand. This ceremony you describe happened in Maine. If it was legal, there will be a record of it, and I will be able to get access to it. Then, if such a record exists, we will know what you will have to do to dissolve the marriage. At least let me check."

"Thank you, Edward. You are truly a good friend. You're right. I need to know what my status is."

It took Edward only a few days to find the answer. "You were never married, Nellie. The state has no record of such a ceremony. And because you left the state and traveled about, there is no way to argue for a common-law marriage. You're free. Always have been."

"A gigantic load just fell from my shoulders, Edward. I've always been afraid that Otis would find me somehow and force me to go back to that marriage. If I had only known that it was a sham all along, I might have made very different choices in my life."

"Well, you know now. Fear of Otis Leath, boy scoundrel, does not need to play a part in the life choices you make from here on in. And now, perhaps, you understand why it is better not to hide the truth."

It was an idyllic time for both of them. Despite a war that seemed as if it might never end, Nellie and Edward looked forward to the future, unafraid of whatever might be coming their way. They were enjoying their lives, their jobs, and each other. That changed one day in early 1865. Nellie perked up when she heard the tapping of Edward's cane, but as he drew closer to her desk she could see that something terrible had happened. His face was white and drawn, as if someone had sucked all the vital juices out of him. Even his eyes were dull.

"Edward! What's wrong?" She jumped up and ran to him, shaking his shoulders to make him look at her.

"My father. He's dead. Dropped dead of a heart attack in his office this morning. I just got the telegram. I have to go home, probably forever. My mother will need me to handle the arrangements. Then there's the office, all his cases and clients. They will all fall to me, even if I don't know what to do with them without him there to advise me. Oh, Nellie, whatever am I going to do?"

"You're going to handle everything. I know you can do it." She wanted to hug him close, but she knew this was not the time. Later, he would need to weep, and she was willing to be there. But right now, he simply needed someone to push him in the right direction.

"Shall I come with you and help you pack? Or would you rather I go and pick up a train ticket for you?"

"I can handle the small stuff here, but I don't know what I'm going to do when I get home—how I'll deal with Mother, how to manage a funeral, settle his affairs."

"Do you want me to come home with you?" She asked the question before she even thought of what it would mean for her own life.

He was staring at her. "You would do that? You said you would never go back to Saco."

"That was in another lifetime, Edward, before I knew there was someone who needed me."

The earth was shaking under their feet as they stared at each other. Then he reached for both her hands and clasped them between his own. "Oh, my dear. You have just given me a greater gift than I ever hoped to receive. But the answer is, 'No, not now.' This is something I have to do on my own. I'll be able to handle it just knowing that you were willing to come."

"But I meant it. I could help with. . ."

"Sh-h-h, Nellie. I want you to come, but I want your home-coming to be a joyous occasion. Let me take care of what I have to do there and take the time to put the raw grief behind me. Then I'll be back to get you, and we'll go home together."

The Civil War that had dominated Nellie Chase's entire adult life ended when General Lee and the Army of Northern Virginia surrendered on April 9, 1865. But for Nellie and Edward, it was just another fluctuation in a sea of changes that were engulfing them. Edward was the executor as well as the principal heir of his father's estate, and the responsibility kept him busy far into the night. Nevertheless, he always found time at the end of the day to send a letter to Nellie. He poured his fears and frustrations onto the paper, hoping that the chain of words would bind her ever closer to him. Those letters revealed parts of his experience that Nellie had not known, and she cherished them for filling in the gaps in her knowledge.

"I'm learning much about my mother," he wrote one day. "I always assumed that she was leading an ideal life, that she enjoyed the position she held as social maven of Saco. But now

I learn that she always wanted to be a farmer. Who would have guessed! She wants to move out of this big house and find a small cottage somewhere, where she and my sisters can live in rooms filled with light, with braided rugs on the floor and a wood stove warming a perpetual pot of soup. She wants a vegetable garden and a chicken coop. Chickens! My mother? But if that is what she wants, then I must do my best to help her find such a place. I'm excited to be in a position to help her fulfill a lifelong dream, but at the same time my heart aches for her when I think of how long she has led a life that she really did not enjoy. Why could she not have told her husband what she has been able to admit to her son? Or did she tell him and he just didn't listen? I hope I am learning some lessons about taking the time to pay attention to the needs of those I love."

Edward did indeed have his hands full. Besides making arrangements for his mother and sisters to move into their new home, he had the family house to worry about. The housekeeper that his parents had employed for as long as he could remember chose this moment to retire. He understood her choice, but at the same time he worried. He needed someone to help with the day-to-day management of the household, but interviewing potential housekeepers was not something he was prepared to do. Kindly, his mother stepped in and volunteered to handle the task for him so that he could concentrate on re-organizing his father's business.

The law offices of Eastman and Son remained open, but there was too much work for a single lawyer and his law clerk to manage. Edward could not yet bring himself to change the gilt letters on the door of the office, but he did try to contact each of his father's clients. He reassured them that he appreciated their business and that the firm stood ready to help them manage their affairs as usual. He reviewed each file, reminding himself of the client's past legal needs, checking to make sure their papers were up to date, noting on his calendar the dates that were most important to each client. He also initiated a search for a young lawyer to bring into the firm. His old law school professor at Dartmouth was happy to do some initial screening and to send him suggestions for his consideration. "I am blessed with people who are willing to help me," he wrote to Nellie. "Yet I miss most of all the chance to talk these decisions over with you."

Nellie, too, was facing major changes. As the war had wound down to its conclusion, the steady steam of patients dried up. Even though Confederate General Stand Watie refused to surrender until June 23, 1865, the War Department in Washington, DC, turned to the difficult task of shutting down much of its military infrastructure. The first closures included military hospitals. Government appointees evaluated the existing patient load at each hospital. The staff submitted the names of those who would continue to need hospitalization and extensive care in the years to come. They were assigned to regional or state medical centers. The remaining patients were to be sent home.

Nellie struggled with the paperwork involved with the transfer of both groups. Finding beds for the long-term care patients was a more difficult task than it sounded, and the patients themselves were feeling great anxiety about what was to become of them. Nellie tried to be as reassuring as she could be, but she could answer few of their questions. They wanted to know where they would be sent, but until she received an acceptance letter from the hospital in their state, she could tell them nothing.

"They look at me with such fear in their eyes," she wrote to Edward. "I've always been the one to reassure them, but I have no reassurances now, and it breaks my heart."

Those who were going home had their own set of worries. All too often, Nellie was reminded of Roger Jamison and his fears that no one would ever be able to love a one-armed man. For many of her ambulatory patients, Steuart Hospital, or Jarvis Hospital as it now was known, had been a sanctuary, a safe haven where they could learn to cope with their disabilities and no one would judge them. Now they would have to face families and friends who did not—could not—understand the experiences they had undergone.

Again and again, Nellie poured out her woes in letters to Edward. "What can I tell someone like Jeremy Hightower? At Appomattox he was assigned stretcher duty on the battlefield. As he bent over to help a wounded comrade, a cannon ball severely wounded him in the buttocks. He has lost so much muscle that he can barely manage to walk with crutches. Now he fears that people will label him as a coward because he was shot from behind. And I suspect that is how he thinks about himself as well. How can I help him through this? I wish I knew, and I wish I had your shoulder to cry on now and then. It would help me to cry, I think, but it's not much comfort to shed tears with no one to wipe them away."

Starting Over

Almost a year after the official end of the war, Jarvis Hospital closed its doors and transferred the last of its patients to local facilities near their homes. Nellie was out of a job. Edward Eastman was there to help her remove the last of her belongings from the small room where she had spent the past three years. "It's time for a decision, Nellie. We'll find you a rooming house on a temporary basis, but you can't hope to stay in Baltimore. It's time for you to come home."

"I don't have a 'home' any more, Edward."

"Yes, you do. Saco is your home and always has been. Your family farm may no longer be there, but the place where you grew up still has a hold on you that you cannot deny. Don't tell me that you do not occasionally dream of those towering pine trees, the waves crashing against the rocky coast line, the Saco River tumbling along its path to the ocean. The Town Square, Trinity Episcopal Church where your family attended services, Mrs. Bennett's Academy for Girls, the County Fair Grounds. Those places formed you, and you can't ever completely escape them."

"That might be true under normal circumstances. It was easy for you to go back because you had never really left the town. But I ran away. I turned my back on the town and the people who lived there. I rejected everything about my former life. I can't now just waltz back in and reclaim something I've repudiated for the past eight years."

"Of course you can. In fact, you offered to do exactly that the day my father died. Do you really think that I have any less need for you to be there because I am no longer actively grieving over his loss?"

"Oh, Edward. We have led such very different lives. We do well together in the bustling urban atmosphere of Baltimore, but in a small town, there would be gossip and people watching my every move to prove that I don't really fit in. I would always be the foolish and rebellious teenager who ran off with the horn player."

"I hate to break that little bubble of an excuse, but you're not that important to most people," Edward told her impatiently. "Look, our country has just gone through a devastating upheaval. We're a nation torn apart by factionalism, and the job of knitting the country back together is not going to be an easy one. Most folks are not going to have the time to chew over the history of little Nellie Chase.

"I want you to marry me, Nellie. We can get married here in Baltimore, so that you are already my wife when you arrive in Saco. I want you to come back to town as Mrs. Edward Eastman, wife of a prominent young lawyer with offices on the Square. You'll move into the Eastman family house on Main Street and take over the role in society that my mother traditionally played before my father's death. She and my two sisters are already settled into her retirement cottage on the edge of town, so we'll have family nearby but not underfoot."

"And people will still want to know who this upstart Mrs. Edward Eastman really is."

"My mother will be a help with that. I've talked about you so much that she says she already feels as if she knows you. As for the others in town, you don't have to tell them your entire life story. That's nobody's business. You are a highly qualified military nurse who served her country for the duration of the war. That's all anyone needs to know. We met in Baltimore, not in Saco, after all. If you don't want anyone to know who you are, that's your decision."

"I'm afraid to marry you, Edward." Nellie was shocked that she could actually say those words, but this was just Edward, after all, the friend to whom she had been able to confess all of her darkest secrets. "I've never been 'in love' and I've never witnessed a truly loving marriage. I don't know what it is that I feel for you, and I can't guarantee that I will always feel the way I do now. How can I make promises when I can't be sure I can keep them?"

"You've lived your life one day at a time, haven't you?"

"Well, I've learned to do that, yes, but . . ."

"So that's how people get through a marriage, too—just one day at a time. We're good friends, Nellie, and beyond that, I happen to be tail over teacups in love with you. I want to wake up each morning knowing that you are there beside me, that no matter what troubles the world has to offer us, we will be strong enough to overcome them, so long as we face those troubles together. I trust you with my life, and I would lay down my life for yours. That's what love is all about, even if you don't recognize it—yet!"

It was destined to be a happy marriage. The year of separation had given both Nellie and Edward the time to hash out their areas of disagreement and to fill in their appreciation of each other as individuals. Nellie's fears that she would be unable to love her new husband evaporated when she walked into her new house for the first time. There, warming herself in a spot of sunlight, was a small calico cat. Her fur was long, and her marking were so distinctly irregular that she looked like a fluffy little clown.

"Oh, Edward," Nellie cried. She fell to her knees and held out her hand. The kitten looked at her and yawned. Then she stretched, one leg after another, before approaching Nellie. She sniffed curiously, and then rubbed the side of her head against Nellie's outstretched hand.

"I think she's saying, 'Welcome home, Momma,'" Edward murmured.

Nellie scooped up the kitten, which was now purring contentedly under Nellie's chin. Struggling to her feet, Nellie threw her free arm around Edward's neck. "I . . . I don't know what to say. I have never received a gift of love like this one."

"Are you talking about the kitten's love?" Edward grinned at her.

"No, yours. You knew exactly what I would need. I can't believe you actually had a cat waiting for me! Oh, she's adorable. Does she have a name?" Nellie's excitement was bubbling over.

"I've been calling her Patches, but you are free to change that. She's your cat."

"Patches is perfect. That's where I found her—in a patch of sunlight—and her fur is in patches, too. Oh, Edward," she cried as the happy tears flowed. The kitten, which was being crushed between them, struggled free and jumped to the floor, where she set about the important task of grooming the fur that Nellie's enthusiasm had ruffled. Nellie laughed through her tears. "The perfect cat. She even knows when to leave us alone!"

⸺✄⸺

Nellie had worried that she would find nothing to do in Saco, but she soon discovered that the end of the war had given birth to a series of philanthropic ventures. The new Wardwell Home for Aged Women provided shelter and care for the widowed wives and mothers of Civil War soldiers. One of Nellie's neighbors, Sarah Fairfield Hamilton, was a champion of women's suffrage and founded the Women's Educational and Industrial Union. Another neighbor, Cornelius Sweetser, left half his estate to charity shortly after Nellie arrived in Saco. His bequests were designated for the creation of a public park, a public high school, and an orphanage. He also left grants to help support the York Institute, dedicated to the cause of education, and the establishment of the Dyer Library.

Each of these organizations offered Nellie an outlet for her organizational talents, and as the wife of a prominent attorney, she was invited to serve on several boards. She shared her medical knowledge with the staffs of both the home for women and the orphanage. She became a familiar visitor, bringing dishes to tempt the appetites of the women and stories to expand the knowledge of the children. Still, she worried that some day someone would recognize her as that silly young girl who had excited a flurry of concern when she ran away from home.

In the fall of 1868, a new threat to her elaborate new identity arose. Edward came home with a hefty book one evening. "Have you seen this?" he asked.

"I don't think so. What is it?" She read the title: *Women of the War: Their Heroism and Self Sacrifice*, by Frank Moore. "What has that to do with me?" But she was already afraid she knew.

"Turn to page 536."

"Nelly M. Chase," she read. "Oh, no. How on earth?"

"This Frank Moore is the son of an military nurse. To honor his mother, he wrote letters to soldiers asking them to tell him about their own favorite nurses on the battlefield. A soldier who chose to remain anonymous apparently sent in the story of a nurse who saved his life at Fredericksburg—you. I'm sorry, Nellie. I thought about keeping this from you, but the book is in our local shop and our friends and neighbors are sure to see it."

"Will they recognize me?"

"I don't know."

"But what if someone recognizes me as that runaway Nellie? I should never have come back to Saco!"

"You don't mean that. You cannot mean that! Nellie, you are my wife, and we have a bountiful life together. Don't wish it away because of a few pages in a book."

"I don't wish to change a moment of it. I only fear that something or someone may attack us from outside, and we won't be able to stop the damage. I would never forgive myself if you became the focus of gossip or ridicule because of something that I did."

Some of their friends did ask whether she was the woman in the book. They knew, of course, that she had been a nurse throughout the war, so they had turned to this popular account to see if she was included. And since there was only one 'Nellie' in the roster of nurses, connecting Nellie Eastman with Nellie Chase was a natural thought. Nellie never denied the question, although she was always reluctant to talk about her days as Nellie Chase. Most of her friends respected that and did not pursue the question. Nor did it strike them as unusual. Almost everyone knew soldiers who could not talk about their experiences, either. What did amaze Nellie was that no one ever asked if she was the same Nellie Chase who once lived in Saco. That was the question Nellie dreaded, but it never came.

"It's not surprising to me, my dear," Edward told her. "I've been telling you that you didn't need to worry."

"But I don't understand. I left here less than ten years ago. People knew my family, knew me, for that matter. Now that they know my maiden name, I would think . . ."

"They don't make the connection, Nellie, because the woman you are is so very different from the child you were. That Nellie was a silly goose of a girl. She wasn't terribly important to anyone back then, except for the grief she caused her parents. That Nellie ran away from home. She probably came to no good end, probably got exactly what was coming to her. That's what they would have thought, if they've thought of that Nellie at all.

"No one, looking at you now, would see anything but a sophisticated and capable woman. Today's Nellie cares unstintingly for others. She is loved by wrinkled old shrews who complain bitterly about the treatment they receive at the hands of every one, with the exception of that lovely young Mrs. Eastman, who always has time for them. And she is equally loved by the small children in the orphanage, who climb into her lap and beg for another one of her wonderful stories.

"That's what you need to accept for yourself, Nellie. Put the child to rest. She is long gone. Then welcome your grown up Nellie and enjoy the full flowering of your personality. When you give up the load of childish guilt you are carrying around, you'll find that all those other grown up burdens are easier to bear."

Part Two: Cuttings From Laura's Story

The story of the Gideonites and the Port Royal Experiment has no lack of colorful characters. Fascinating people inhabit all kinds of exotic scenery—swamps, pluff mud, tropical vegetation, glorious sunrises, and sandy ocean beaches. It has drama—a background of America's Civil War, heroic acts of bravery, enormous pain and suffering, and a life-changing struggle for freedom.

While I was writing *The Road to Frogmore*, I listed all the names of real people with whom Laura Towne came in contact during her first years in South Carolina. There turned out to be hundreds of them—and most of those had to go. I examined both individuals and groups, always asking the same question: Did this person help or hinder Laura in a significant way? If the answer was yes, the character stayed. But if I could not make a case for individuals as significant, I killed their characters, no matter how fascinating their personal stories seemed.

The members of the Roundhead Regiment, including Nellie Chase and her small family of soldiers and ex-slaves, were some of my favorite, but unnecessary, characters. True, they were in Beaufort when Laura arrived. The Roundheads and the Gideonites met on several occasions. Laura and Nellie had a few similar slave encounters. But there is no evidence that Nellie influenced Laura in any way. That they reached somewhat similar conclusions speaks only to the validity of those conclusions. Although I have had readers of *A Scratch with the Rebels* and *Beyond All Price* ask for more about these characters, they had already had their moments in the sun. This new book was not their story.

Robert Smalls lived an amazing life for a slave. He had a connection with Laura's companions, the Gideonites, because his wife and children lived at Coffin Point, the plantation run by Edward Philbrick. Laura visited often, bringing medical care to the freedmen there, and when Smalls pulled off his great act of derring-do, I'm sure Laura was among those who cheered him. But while others of the Gideonites hustled Smalls off to Washington to show that a slave could do great things for the country, his accomplishments had no permanent effect on Laura or the children in Laura's classroom. This was not his story, either.

The Gideonites were a diverse group of people. A total of seventy-three northerners traveled to South Carolina in the spring of 1862, all determined in one way or another to prove the rightness of the abolitionist cause. They were socialites and sheltered spinsters, old and young, teachers, ministers, lawyers, philanthropists, and failed businessmen. And they all had back-stories that explained why they gave up everything to risk this venture. How could I ignore the spiritual leader of the group who found himself on trial as an embezzler? The opera singer with seven children who wrote such lurid prose that she could almost be classified as a pornographer? The cotton agent who beat one of the other Gideonites to a battered and bloody wreck? The wealthy socialite who could not lower herself to do actual work of any kind? The free black teacher who confounded everyone because they expected to see a clear line of color separation between teachers and students.

The Gideonites as a group are worthy of study, and as individuals their stories make great reading. Once again, my reasons for choosing to feature some of them and ignore others depended on the impact they had on Laura and her goal. If they played a crucial role in the plot, they stayed. If they went home early or had nothing to contribute to the main story, I excluded them.

.

Salmon P. Chase's Slave Problem

S almon P. Chase was a beleaguered man. As Lincoln's new Secretary of the Treasury, he had thought himself capable of bringing his considerable training and educational background to bear on managing the civilian side of the war. He had not, however, anticipated having quite so many problems dumped in his lap all at once.

The South Carolina Expeditionary Force was a joint Army-Navy venture under the leadership of General Thomas W. Sherman and Commander Samuel F. DuPont. Their mission—to establish a safe harbor from which to manage the blockade of the southern coast—had been a tremendous logistical exercise. Eighty ships and 12,000 troops needed much financial support from the government, but Lincoln had simply instructed Chase to "get it done." And so he had. When dispatches came back reporting the unqualified success of the Battle of Port Royal, Chase had celebrated along with everyone else.

"Who would have thought that the Confederate forces would just give up that easily?" he pointed out to the young clerks in his office. "We thought they had Port Royal Harbor well-fortified. Instead, it turned out that they had less than 200 men there, and only a few operable guns, not one of which was able to swivel to attack a passing ship. It seems almost too easy."

"The civilians, too. Is it true, sir, that they just hightailed it out of the islands when they heard we were coming?"

"Apparently so. I've just received a copy of a report from Mr. H. T. Boyd, a civilian who delivered supplies to the Port Royal fortifications. He was aboard the Confederate steamer *General Clinch,* on his way with supplies for Hilton Head and Bay Point. When the invasion began, the *General Clinch* fled for the safety of the city of Beaufort, where the crew found the people of the city preparing to abandon their homes for the safety of the mainland. Catching some of their fever, Boyd decided that it might be safer to move all of his Beaufort records and supplies back onto his ship. While he was making arrangements to do so, the panicked citizens stormed the boat and loaded it with their own goods. The captain, fearing that his ship was already dangerously overloaded, only offered to take the paper records belonging to the Quartermaster's Corps. Instead, Boyd and the Quartermaster attempted to carry the papers to safety in Pocotaligo in two mule carts. Hearing more rumors there, they thought about returning to Beaufort to rescue more public documents, but the mules were unfit for more travel, no horses were available, and they abandoned the plan. Instead, they retreated to Charleston."

"That must have been quite a sight—all those folks fighting to get aboard a small steamer."

"And remember, panic engenders more panic. Throw in a bunch of screaming children, some family pets, and a few hysterical women. If I'd have been that ship captain, I'd have just sailed away and left them all stranded."

"I'm glad he didn't," Secretary Chase commented. "I suspect the whole episode falls into the category of good riddance. They did leave behind some problems, however. They didn't just move out of the city of Beaufort. They abandoned their plantations with all the land they owned. They abandoned the cotton crop, which was just ready for harvest. And, for the most part, they abandoned their slaves."

"Really? They didn't take their slaves with them?"

"Some took their personal slaves, and others dragooned a few of their men to drive their wagons and row the boats they were using to escape. But General Sherman reports that there are hundreds, maybe thousands, of Negroes hiding in the interior of Hilton Head Island. And blacks have overrun Beaufort, from all reports, rioting and breaking into the lovely mansions there to steal and ransack. The slave owners are gone, and the worst fears of what might happen if the slaves were freed seem to be coming true. There's simply no one to control them."

The problem of what to do with the black population of the Sea Islands had frustrated General Sherman almost from the moment of his arrival. The able-bodied blacks had come to the Army looking for employment, and Sherman had tried to put them to work. But along with them came their families— wives, children, and aged parents—all needing food, clothing, and medical attention. He had repeatedly requested that the government make a policy decision on paying the former slaves to work the deserted plantations and that teachers and supervisors be sent to deal with the problem.

Lincoln's government was not ready to emancipate the former slaves. The president wanted to see them treated humanely, but he also understood that the stability of his own office depended upon pacifying the Border States, populated by those who were slave-owners as well as those who were not. Thus, while the slavery question loomed over nearly every government decision, no one seemed willing to offer more than platitudes when pressed for a solution. Southerners watching events from Charleston recognized that the needs of the former slaves were enormous—more than the "gentlemen of large expectations and liberal ideas" were equipped to handle.

According to Sherman's estimates, there were at least 9000 blacks on Hilton Head, "daily increasing in numbers and daily diminishing in their resources . . ." The official army description, forwarded to headquarters by General Sherman, failed to recognize the promise of the slave farms. "Hordes of totally uneducated, ignorant, and improvident blacks have been abandoned by their constitutional guardians," he wrote, "not only to all the future chances of anarchy and starvation, but in such a state of abject ignorance and mental stolidity as to preclude all possibility of self-government and self-maintenance in their present condition."

Other observers of the South Carolina coast saw that huge amounts of money could be had from the abandoned cotton crops. True, some plantation owners had burned their fields and warehouses to keep the crop from falling into enemy hands, but not all had had time to do so. Much of the crop grown in 1861 was still available if someone could get it harvested and coordinate its sale and shipment. There was also a certain amount of urgency involved in the need to replant. Fields were lying fallow and the labor was available. If a new cotton crop could be seeded by mid-February, the profits would go a long way toward financing the army and feeding the black workers at the same time.

"Well, are these abandoned slaves actually free now?" asked another clerk.

"Nobody seems to be quite sure," Chase replied. "There's been no official declaration from the government that they have been freed, and I don't expect one. But there's a difference between official policy and events of the moment. The image that keeps coming to mind—degrading as it may sound—is that of a herd of cattle suddenly finding an open gate and starting a stampede. They're out of their pen and behaving as if they are free, but they are still domestic beasts who have to be rounded up."

"So who's going to corral them?"

"I have no idea. I just hope it's not this office."

But of course it was Secretary Chase's problem. The deserted plantations, the abandoned cotton crop, and the ownerless slaves—all were considered the spoils of war and came into the hands of the Department of the Treasury. Just months earlier, General Benjamin F. Butler had set a precedent at Fort Monroe in Virginia when he sheltered three runaway slaves, calling them "contraband of war." It was a convenient term, having the distinction of being backed by international law. It meant that former slaves who came into the territory held by the U. S. Army could be protected, even though they were not legally free. Like it or not, the Expeditionary Force had ended up in possession of nearly ten thousand slaves, and by labeling them as contraband, the slaves became the property of the federal government.

In early December, Chase invited several of his friends and political allies to a working lunch meeting at the Willard Hotel in Washington D.C. Among the attendees were Senator Charles Sumner from Massachusetts; Senator Benjamin Wade from Ohio; Congressman Owen Lovejoy from Illinois; William Lloyd Garrison, editor of *The Liberator,* an anti-slavery newspaper; and Horace Greeley, founder and editor of *The New York Tribune.* All of these men were sincere advocates of abolition; all could be counted upon to offer good advice as to what ought to be done about the problems in South Carolina.

After a comfortable repast of roast beef and potatoes, Chase leaned back in his chair, lit a cigar, and pronounced, "Gentlemen, I need your help."

"I presume you're referring to the problems at Port Royal," Sumner said. "I've always heard it said that one should be careful about making a wish before thinking about what the outcome might be. This might definitely be one of those instances."

"Meaning we got more than we bargained for when we invaded South Carolina," Lovejoy added.

"We certainly did. No one expected the entire citizenry of the Sea Islands to flee for the mainland, leaving everything behind. So now I have a desk full of problems. We have possession of a great deal of land, a cotton crop that northern manufacturers need, but one that is in danger of being lost, and 10,000 contraband slaves. How do I handle all of this, gentlemen? You've all preached the need to free the country of the stain of slavery. Now that I have the opportunity, how do I go about it?"

"Port Royal was just one battle. I don't think you're going to solve the problems until we win the war." Senator Wade shook his head and shrugged.

"These problems can't wait, Benjamin. I have to act now. But I don't want to move until I am sure that whatever I do will not jeopardize the abolitionist movement. That's why I've called you here."

"Is the land that valuable?"

"Potentially, yes. This is good, fertile soil, and the plantations have supported a wealthy gentleman farmer's society for decades. The city of Beaufort is one of the cultural garden spots of the South. The whole area could be a source of enormous income if it is handled correctly. I can't let it slip through our fingers."

"But the Army's in charge of it at the moment, are they not?"

"Yes, of course. And they need much of the land to support the defenses they are setting up there. There is, however, the danger of destroying the land so that it cannot be restored to other uses once the war is over. Then, too, we may need the cropland that is available there. If we could turn the abandoned plantations into producing farms, they could solve a huge logistical problem of transporting food supplies from the North to the South."

"What about the cotton crop that's there now? Why hasn't it been harvested by now?"

"Because there's no one there to harvest it. The plantation owners hadn't gotten around to it, because cotton can sit in the fields for a long time before it's harvested. But eventually winter weather will beat it down. And now there's also a threat of fire. Our pickets have caught a couple of owners sneaking back to their land to put a torch to the fields. They know they can't get the crop for themselves. All they can do is try to deny it to our use."

CAROLYN P. SCHRIBER

"So why aren't we harvesting it?"

"The answer to that comes out sounding like a defense of slavery, so you will have to pardon me for a moment if I sound like an advocate of slave labor." Secretary Chase sighed. "Picking cotton is grueling, backbreaking work. You can't ask soldiers to do it. Slaves pick cotton only when someone with a whip is standing over them. And at the moment, the available slaves are all rejoicing in the wonderful news that they don't have to pick cotton anymore."

"Would they do it if they were paid?" Horace Greeley asked. "I've seen the figures, and I understand how valuable that crop is. Surely it would be worth it to our government to offer the contrabands a salary to go back and do the things they know how to do."

"That's what I'm considering," Chase agreed. "But I need someone to take charge. Someone I can send down there to organize the slaves and show them that they can improve their lot in life by working for us. It also needs to be someone with a working knowledge of the cotton markets, someone who could oversee the whole process of getting the cotton from field to manufacturer. Who do you know that fits that description, gentlemen?"

"Right off hand, I can't come up with anyone, but let us think about it. Maybe one of us will have a sudden brilliant idea. In the mean time, though, I don't see how getting the cotton crop picked gets us any closer to solving the real problems of the Negro, Salmon."

Garrison had been sitting quietly and listening to the discussion. But now his abolitionist ardor took over. "I've had correspondence from Admiral DuPont," he said. "He reports that the Negroes there are starving because the Army has confiscated all their food supplies for their own use. He says they have no clothes for the winter because their owners have always supplied them, and now those owners are gone. They have no doctors—never did have, except for care provided by the plantation mistress. They have no one to lead church services or read the Bible to them. They can't read or write or cipher because it has been against South Carolina law to teach them how to do so. They are flocking into the military camps, hoping for some kind of help, but the Army is not equipped to handle them. It's a disaster in the making. And if we are responsible for the deaths of all those people, I for one will never forgive myself—or my government."

"You've wrapped it up perfectly, William. That's my problem, too. And again, I need someone who can go down there, assess the needs of the Negro population, and bring back recommendations as to what we do next."

"I've heard rumors that President Lincoln is going to ask Congress to find somewhere else for the Negroes to go," Lovejoy said. "He supposedly has some sort of colonization plan to send them away to a climate where they would be more comfortable."

"Where? Like a jungle?" Garrison snorted in derision.

"No, that rumor has been around for a long time. The slaves themselves have told the soldiers that their owners predicted they would all be sent off to Cuba. That's not going to happen. The contrabands are going to stay where they are, and we have to find someone to deal with them. Again, whom do you know? I need an agent to deal with the economic problems and a philanthropist to handle the human needs."

Reynolds and Pierce

No immediate answers came out of the meeting that afternoon, but help was on the way. Just a few days later, Lieutenant Colonel William H. Reynolds arrived at Secretary Chase's office. He introduced himself as a member of the First Rhode Island Artillery, and handed Chase an introductory letter from William Sprague, the new governor of Rhode Island. Chase immediately recognized the writer as the wealthy young politician who was courting Chase's daughter. Impressed by that connection, Chase read that Reynolds had extensive experience in the cotton trade, that he was honest, highly principled, and fervently religious.

"Colonel, you are the answer to a prayer," he said. "Are you willing to leave immediately? The cotton situation is one of pressing urgency."

"Yes, sir. I can leave tomorrow morning. Just tell me what you want me to do."

"Your first—perhaps your only—consideration should be to get the cotton crop in as quickly as possible, before winter rain or rebel firebrands render it useless. I believe that General

Sherman has already made some initial efforts to recruit the former slaves on each plantation to pick the cotton in exchange for a small salary. But you will have to organize them, set supervisors over them, make arrangements to gin the cotton, and ship it North. And there's no time to waste."

"I understand, sir. It shouldn't be a problem, except, perhaps, for the ginning. What is the condition of the gins there? And are there people who can operate them?"

"Well, from what I hear, many of the gins have been destroyed, either by their former owners who didn't want us to get our hands on them or by the slaves who never wanted to work them again. However, it's not a particularly complicated piece of machinery. You should be able to manage quick repairs if necessary."

"And do I have permission to do that, sir? I mean, may I requisition whatever tools and materials I need to get the job done?"

"Certainly. I'll have your orders drawn up this afternoon. They will give you full permission to confiscate anything you may need to get that harvest in."

"Thank you, sir. I won't let you down." Snapping an unnecessary but impressive salute, Reynolds turned on a military heel and hurried off to arrange his passage.

If Salmon P. Chase had been a superstitious man, he might have paused to suspect that the arrangement had been all too easy. Upon some reflection, he realized that young Reynolds had voiced no concern for the Negroes he was going out to organize. His interest had only been in how far he would be allowed to go to achieve his purposes. Still, Chase had asked for a cotton agent, and to find one with a reputation for honesty might have been more than he could have asked for.

Colonel Reynolds arrived in Beaufort on December 20, 1861, and set to work in a whirlwind of activity that soon antagonized most of those with whom he was supposed to be cooperating. He cut the salary that General Sherman had promised each slave, while informing the slaves that they had made an unbreakable contract to work for him. He further reduced the amount of cash layout by making the salaries partially payable in food and clothing. Had anyone asked, he would have said he was taking care of the slaves, making sure they had their basic needs met before handing them money to fritter away. To himself, he might have admitted that his eye was only on the bottom line of profit he would be able to claim.

It didn't take him long to antagonize the Army, either. Reynolds took his orders literally. He had been given permission to confiscate anything he needed to complete his mission. He interpreted that with a strong emphasis on the 'anything'. He claimed a plantation house for the use of each of his plantation supervisors, arguing that living in 'the big house' would command more respect and obedience from the slaves who were used to having a 'Massa'. He also made sure that each of those houses had the finest furnishings and equipment available. Of course, soldiers assigned to guard various parts of the Low Country had already occupied many of the choicest plantations. No matter. Brandishing his orders from Secretary Chase, he sent the soldiers packing so that he could move his own men in.

His worst offense, according to General I. I. Stevens, commander of the 2nd Brigade, was seizing the Beaufort Public Library. Stevens had seen that library as a source of healthful recreation and continuing education for his young soldiers. He had sent them in to clean it up and put it back in operation. Reynolds countermanded the order, had the books packed up, and sent them North, where they were to be sold to raise money to transport his cotton. Stevens fumed and vowed to refuse all further cooperation with the arrogant cotton agent.

Meanwhile, Salmon P. Chase continued his search for someone to concentrate on the welfare of the former slaves. In further consultation with Senator Sumner, he decided to approach a mutual friend, Edward L. Pierce. Senator Sumner had pointed out an article written by the young Pierce and published in the November issue of *The Atlantic Monthly*. Earlier that year, Pierce had been serving a three-month enlistment at Fort Monroe, and thus had been able to observe how General Butler had handled the contrabands. Pierce had been duly impressed with the eagerness of the former slaves to learn to read and to serve their country. They were fully capable as well as deserving of American citizenship, Pierce had argued.

Chase contacted Pierce by mail, asking if he would be willing to postpone opening his planned law practice in Boston long enough to travel to South Carolina and assess the needs of the former slaves there. Pierce agreed to spend several more months in the service of his government before becoming a practicing attorney. He left New York on January 13, 1862, and was soon hard at work, traveling from plantation to plantation to learn about the former slaves and their current condition.

Although he had initially hoped that he could work closely with the cotton agents, he soon realized that he and Colonel Reynolds had very different goals. Pierce wanted whatever was best for the Negro; Reynolds cared only for what was best for the cotton crop. The two men watched each other carefully while managing to avoid most arguments about what they believed. However, on one issue, Edward Pierce found it impossible to control his anger.

"Colonel Reynolds. Is it true that you are arranging to ship all the cotton North to be ginned there?"

"I'm not sure why that should matter to you, but, yes, that's exactly what I'm going to do."

"But the slaves could easily do that work, and they need the income."

"They can't gin cotton if they've destroyed the cotton gins," Reynolds said.

"The slaves say the plantation owners were the ones who jammed the gins, and they are willing to help do the repairs and get the machinery back in working order. There's no need to ship the cotton off."

"It will save us money and time. Both are important."

"But the welfare of the slaves is important, too. They can learn to take care of themselves, but they need employment. You're taking away the only jobs they know how to do."

"Then let them learn to work at something else."

"That will take more time than repairing the gins." Edward was dimly aware that this was becoming a childish argument, but he was helpless to control his indignation. "Besides," he said, "there's a more important consideration. If the cotton has to be ginned in the North, you'll lose all the seed from this year's crop."

"So what? We can always order more seed for next year."

"Not this long-staple seed, you can't. Nobody sells it."

"Nonsense."

"It's not nonsense. The high value of Low Country cotton depends on its quality. And that quality has long been determined by the careful cultivation of the seed crop from year to year, using only the seed from the finest products. Nowhere else do you find cotton with such naturally long fibers. It produces a stronger thread and a smoother fabric. And it grows well only in fields like these, with long hot days and cool nights, and the unique fertilizer that comes from the muck the slaves dig up from the marshes."

"Well, well, well! Who turned you into an cotton expert?"

"The same people whose livelihoods you are threatening—the slaves who work this land. If you send the unginned cotton North, the seeds will be lost. Long-staple cotton won't grow well anywhere but here, and the seeds you buy from a catalog will not produce the same quality of cotton that buyers are used to."

"Then that's the way it will have to be. I'm not concerned with keeping these ex-slaves growing cotton for the rest of their lives, and neither should you be. I've been sent to get this crop to market as quickly as possible, and that's what I intend to do. You have no orders to overrule me, so why don't you run along and worry about teaching the darkies their ABCs."

Edward Pierce might have given up his efforts then and there, had it not been for the arrival of an ally. The Reverend Mansfield French of New York City had applied to Secretary Chase for permission to visit the islands and determine what the American Missionary Association might be able to do to help the Negroes. Chase and French had known each other when they were both living in Ohio and involved in educational efforts. They had even worked together to raise money to establish Wilberforce University for Negroes there. Chase welcomed French to the cause and sent him off shortly after Pierce departed from New York.

Mansfield and Pierce were very different in age and religious convictions, but they shared some traits that were even more important—compassion for the downtrodden and impatience with the self-serving. They agreed to return home and begin the implementation of a long-range plan to bring about full emancipation. Their plan neatly superseded the need for cotton agents by stressing the Negroes' own knowledge of cotton cultivation, their eagerness to learn, and their willingness to work for reasonable wages under proper, benevolent supervision. They envisioned a management system that would give guidance to independent farmers and assist only with those aspects of the cotton trade that would be temporarily out of the reach of the uneducated. Both planned to recruit a band of teachers and religious leaders who would come to the South to help the slaves grow into full and productive citizenship. They meant to prove that the Negro would work and even fight for his freedom and for his country. It was an idealistic dream, but one that abolitionists would flock to support.

Pierce returned to Boston in mid-February, and immediately gained the support of Reverend Jacob Manning, a minister at the Old South Church. Manning agreed to recruit missionaries and teachers to go back to South Carolina. He also promised to raise the money to support them, so that they would not be answerable to the federal government. Meanwhile, Reverend Mansfield was doing the same thing in New York City. Within days the two had established The New York National Freedmen's Relief Association and the Boston Educational Association for Freedmen. While Colonel Reynolds sought to accomplish his immediate goals, French and Pierce dreamed larger dreams.

Gideon's Army

Edward L. Pierce spent only a short time in Port Royal during January 1862, but he immediately realized that his goals and those of Reynolds were bound to conflict. Returning home fired by the need to rescue the former slaves through education, he turned to two organizations, the newly founded Boston Educational Commission for Freedmen and the American Missionary Society headquartered in New York. As he later described his goals, he sought people who would be dedicated to "the industrial, social, intellectual, moral and religious elevation of persons released from Slavery in the course of the War for the Union." Working together, the two groups screened applicants and chose a band of fifty-three people willing to sail to Port Royal and do what they could to help. They departed from New York on March 3, 1862, and arrived in Beaufort on March 9.

The group of teachers and missionaries who would become known as "Gideon's Band" had assembled for the first time on Friday evening, March 2, at the home of the tax collector for the Port of New York. There, the tax collector had agreed to administer to each of them the wartime "Oath of Allegiance" and to issue them their passports. For several of the group, the realization that they were headed out of the United States and into what was now another country came as a shock. A voyage to South Carolina had not seemed far away; many of them had made that trip before. But now it was considered a foreign country and they needed passports? That was new, and frightening.

The twenty-five men from Boston were almost uniformly Unitarian, between the ages of twenty and twenty-five, well-educated in the local law, medical, or divinity schools, and, if they were not known abolitionists, they had been screened to make sure they had no sympathy for slavery. Edward Pierce had handpicked them from over 150 applicants. The men from New York, however, tended to be older, more experienced in the ways of the world, and more evangelical in their religious beliefs. Some might have assumed that Pierce and French had each chosen those who most resembled themselves.

William Channing Garrett was just twenty-two when he joined this band. He had recently graduated from Harvard and was struggling with a need to do something beneficial to the war effort, even though his Unitarian father was too much a pacifist to allow his son to become a soldier. In his diary, he described his companions as a strange mixture of "clerks, doctors, divinity-students; professors and teachers, underground railway agents and socialists . . . white hairs and black . . . Unitarians, free-thinkers, Methodists, straitlaced, and the other Evangelical sects."

Edward Philbrick, a Boston engineer, admitted that some of his fellow missionaries "look like broken-down schoolmasters" and worried about their practical abilities. Others saw them as distinctly seedy. John Murray Forbes, an industrialist from Boston, was a passenger on the same ship. He described them as ". . . odd-looking men, with odder-looking women." He was not sure "whether it was the adjournment of a John Brown meeting or the fag end of a broken-down phalanstery . . ."

Twelve ladies had joined the group, somewhat to the displeasure of Edward L. Pierce, who had never given a thought to taking anyone but men. Reverend Mansfield French, however, had insisted on taking his wife along, and that had opened the door for other women from New York City and Boston who also applied to go.

The self-appointed leader of the Gideonite women was Austa French, wife of Mansfield French. Her husband was a Methodist minister and early proponent of the theory that ex-slaves should be educated and trained to take full part in the privileges of citizenship. Mansfield and Austa were among the first group of missionaries and teachers sent to South Carolina from New York by the National Freedmen's Relief Association. Austa was in many ways a Yankee superwoman. Highly educated, prominent in society, a singer with operatic training, the mother of seven children, an experienced teacher, and a writer—she set out at the age of 52 to spread the gospel of abolitionism. And "gospel" it was to her. She prided herself on having grown to be an evangelical pastor's wife after her fairly restrained Congregationalist background. Her "calling" during the Civil War was to reveal the evils of slavery to the people of the North.

Her companions quickly noticed her unrestrained enthusiasm, her volubility, her humorless determination that the rest of the world would surely come to see things her way, if she could just lecture them long and hard enough. Historians who write about her tend to describe her (and her husband, too) as the people the rest of the Gideonites would have liked to slap. Drawing no distinctions between outright crimes, actions of which she disapproved, religious beliefs she did not share, and mistakes that needed gentle correction, she was given to loud public denunciations of all behaviors that irritated her. (And it took very little to irritate her, as Susan Walker learned the evening she was too tired from her labors to kneel during one of Austa's interminable prayers.)

Austa loved slaves indiscriminately. She was known to greet a new black acquaintance by throwing her arms around her neck, weeping on her shoulder, and calling her "my sister" before she had even learned the woman's name. But as for the rest of the world, few of her associates lived up to her standards. She was quick to refer to "the dirty Irish," "white trash," "greedy cotton agents," and "thugs in military uniforms." And she hated South Carolina, pointing to the Spanish moss, the swamps, and the huge black crows as evidence of the evil that permeated every inch of the lands that had harbored slavery.

Then there was her book: *Slavery in South Carolina*. She began writing it almost immediately upon her arrival in Beaufort, long before she had had time or experience to inform her writing. She encouraged the slaves to compete with each other in telling her the most lurid stories of atrocities committed against them. To be fair to Austa, there is no evidence that she made up any of the stories on her own. She simply recorded what she was told. If she picked and chose among the details, however, it was only to be sure she included all the tales with some sexual component or gory physical details. For a devout Christian missionary, she skirted very close to the edge of writing pornography. Austa did a fairly good job of casting shadows on her own character.

Socialite Susan Walker was traveling as a companion of Reverend and Mrs. French, but her purposes could not have been more different. Salmon P. Chase had insisted on sending Miss Susan Walker along to serve as his eyes and ears. In her obituary, someone described her as: "a philanthropist, politician, mathematician, abolitionist, strong-minded woman . . . of somewhat masculine appearance, with a large frame, dominated by a powerful intellect, and unusually quick sympathies." While the Frenches were fervent evangelical missionaries, Susan Walker was a Unitarian abolitionist.

Susan was the only daughter among several sons in a prominent and well-to-do Massachusetts family. She had had a first-rate education and was also a world traveler. She counted among her friends most well known Boston abolitionists, as well as many of the leading politicians serving in Lincoln's government. She was on first-name terms with Salmon P. Chase, Secretary of the Treasury; William H. Seward, Secretary of State; Edwin M. Stanton, Secretary of War; Senator Charles Sumner of Massachusetts; and Governor John A. Andrew of Massachusetts. In fact, on this trip, she carried a special charge: to report directly to Chase on the successes and failure of the mission.

Susan had trouble from the start, finding no common ground among the other missionaries. The two women, Austa and Susan, represented opposite side of a battle that pitted an intellectual against an evangelical and hindered everything that the teacher-missionaries tried to do. Susan's reactions to the realities of a slave-based culture reveal deep-seated and erroneous northern assumptions about the nature of the slave population.

Voyage

On Saturday morning, Susan Walker arrived early to board the steamer Atlantic. She had no patience with people who arrived late to any affair, with the result that she herself was usually distressingly early. This time, only Austa and Mansfield French had arrived earlier, so the three of them stood together for a while making the sort of uncomfortable small talk one engages in with strangers.

"We seemed to make a congenial group last evening," Austa said. "I do hope everyone will get along."

"I'm sure we will. After all, we're all dedicated to the same cause," Susan responded.

Austa gave a small shrug of her shoulders. "Well, one always has a few reservations about people one does not know well. For example, some of those young Bostonians with their scruffy beards. I thought they looked more than a little silly, as if they were playing at being grown-ups. They didn't exactly inspire my confidence."

"Beards are just the current style in Boston," Susan said.

"Well, we usually keep well up with 'style' in New York, and I assure you that our men remain clean-shaven," Austa replied.

"Oh, Austa, if that's all you have to complain about, we should consider ourselves most fortunate," her husband said patiently. "Besides I assure you that those beards won't last long in South Carolina. Just wait till the young fops meet the 'no-see-ums'."

"The 'no-see-ums'? What are they? Some sort of street gang?"

"See. There you go again, being overly suspicious, my dear."

"Well, it sounds frightening to me, too," Susan said. "What are 'no-see-ums'?"

"They are insects, ladies. Such tiny ones that you really can't see them. At most, you may notice a tiny speck of dust. But by the next morning, you find that they have left you an itchy welt out of all proportion to their size. They don't play fair. At least a mosquito is large enough to see, and you have a fair shot at being able to swat him before he bites. But these little fellows are sneaky until the damage is done. Then you will think they have huge fangs."

"Where'd you hear of them?"

"I had the dubious privilege of meeting them myself when I went down there last month. Nasty business, I tell you, and those gentlemen with their beards will get the worst of it."

"Why is that?" Susan asked. "Do they particularly have a taste for men?"

"No, it's the facial hair I worry about. You see, the swarms of 'no-see-ums' live in the garlands of Spanish moss that decorate all the trees down there. And Spanish moss looks amazingly like curly facial hair. So they are likely to swarm into a gentleman's beard looking for a home, and they'll discover one that comes with a warm blood supply. No, those beards will be coming off within a day, I suspect. You ladies enjoy your day, now. I must be off to see if I can help with the loading."

Susan wasn't sure whether she should believe Reverend French or not, so she attempted to bring the topic of conversation back to the nature of the group as a whole. "I was pleased to see that everyone is eager to get to work among the newly-freed slaves. I'm sure that as long as we have a unity of purpose, we'll have no problems with a lack of congeniality."

"I do hope you are correct," Austa said, in a tone that suggested she thought nothing of the sort. "It did seem to me, however, that there was some tendency for certain individuals to cling to those who share their city of origin or their mutual church affiliation."

"Ah, but that's normal, don't you think? We all prefer the things with which we are most familiar."

"Perhaps. But it won't do for us to be bringing the Word of God to the Negro if we don't all agree on the nature of that Word."

Susan frowned. "I saw no evidence of discord or hostility to anyone's religion. Did I miss something?"

"I certainly received a less than enthusiastic response when I invited some of those young men to join my husband and me for worship every evening. Mr. French does the preaching, and I lead the hymn singing. You'll be joining us, I know."

"Ah, Mrs. French, you and your husband are evangelical Methodists, I understand. And many of the Bostonians are members of the Unitarian Church. It may be that your preference for fervent religious expression are rather too emotional for people of other faiths."

"There's only one true faith, and that is Christianity. I don't believe in letting people just go off and establish new churches whenever they find something they don't agree with."

"Excuse me, Mrs. French, but didn't the Methodists split off from the Episcopal Church in England?" Susan knew she was being provocative, but she couldn't help herself. "I'm a Unitarian myself, and we find that it is best not to emphasize our differences but rather our common beliefs in equality, justice, and compassion."

"Mr. French has been charged with being the spiritual leader of this expedition, and that is exactly how he will behave. Anyone who doesn't accept his guidance is still free to decide not to accompany us to do God's work in South Carolina."

"Please. I wasn't questioning his leadership. But it seems to me that so long as we are all dedicated to the same Christian ideals, it shouldn't matter how we choose to worship. Bringing food, clothing, and basic education to the Negro should not be limited to those who attend your daily prayer meetings." Susan was already a very tall woman, but when she drew herself up in indignation and stared down the length of her long and sharp nose, she seemed to loom over the tiny woman opposing her.

Austa French responded with a glare and stomped away. Susan sighed as her shoulders relaxed. I'm off to a fine start, she scolded herself. That little woman will never forget this day, and she will never forgive me. I just did what I said Unitarians did not do. I questioned her beliefs and emphasized our differences. But she was doing the same thing. The only difference is that I feel rather ashamed, and I don't think she does.

As the rest of Gideon's Band began to arrive, the weather turned nasty. A cold wind whistled through the harbor, and huge raindrops spattered on those waiting to board the ship. The tax collector was there again, trying to swear in anyone who had missed the previous evening's gathering, and the ship's captain was making one last check of everyone's paperwork. The wind and rain were not helpful in making either of those activities run smoothly.

Meanwhile porters bumped and dodged their way through the crowd, loading not only luggage, but also huge stores of food and used clothing. Chaos reigned. In a particularly unpleasant incident, Miss Mena Hale, one of the New York ladies, was discovered not to be carrying her necessary documentation. When the captain told her she could not board without all her papers, she burst into tears.

"You can't make me go back and try to find all those papers," she wailed. "My father didn't want me to go on this trip in the first place, and if I go home now, he'll just try to stop me again."

"Then perhaps it might be best if you did not go just now," suggested Mr. Pierce as he pushed his way through the crowd. "We don't want this experiment in Christian charity to cause any family discord. I think you should go on home and take more time to think about this decision."

"No! I won't! Why do you all want to get rid of me? Do you think I can't do the job because I'm a woman?" she demanded of Mr. Pierce.

"That has nothing to do with the issue, Miss Hale. But we can't let you travel without proper papers. You could be stranded in enemy territory with no way to get home again. We can't take that chance."

Mr. Pierce reached to take her arm, but she swatted at him with her small valise. "Take your hands off of me! What do you think you are doing?"

"What's going on here?" another female voice shouted. Austa French pushed her way through the crowd. She was still angry from her discussion with Susan Walker. A red flush bloomed over her face, and she was fairly spitting with indignation. "You men unhand this woman immediately. I know her. She's part of our delegation from New York City and a member of Reverend French's own congregation. She was in our meeting last night, and no one questioned her then. I will personally vouch for her, and anyone who tries to stop her boarding will answer to me."

It was an inauspicious start for the Port Royal Experiment, and conditions did not improve. The little ship turned out to be poorly equipped for normal passenger travel. There were not enough separate quarters for the ladies, and no comfortable place to sit or lie down on deck.

The storm grew worse, adding high waves to the mix and tossing the *Atlantic* about with abandon. Most passengers were immediately seasick and scrambled for the railings to relieve themselves of their last meal. Someone suggested that everyone go below, but the fetid air and close quarters soon drove most of them back to the main deck. The crew handed out waterproof sheets to give the passengers some protection, but by then most of them were beyond caring. They simply huddled together in misery.

If Mrs. French had worried that there would not be enough praying going on aboard the ship, she was wrong. Everyone prayed, although many of those prayers were for a mercifully quick death. Now and then, when the wind died a bit, someone tried to get everyone to join in singing a hymn, but the results were thin and, according to Susan Walker, more than a little discordant.

Arrival in the Low Country

Four days passed before the small ship reached South Carolina. The sight of land was welcome, although the scenery particularly impressed no one. The salt marches and sea oats seemed to stretch forever, and the military encampment on Hilton Head Island had stripped the landscape of much of its natural vegetation. Rows of tents, piles of weapons, and grubby soldiers did not provide much encouragement.

Nor were the missionaries able to disembark from their tiny ship. There were no accommodations for them, and Mr. Pierce made the decision that everyone could stay aboard the *Atlantic* for one more night. In resignation, they all settled down again on the deck. In the morning, they learned that the *Atlantic* had too deep a draft to make the trip up the Broad River to the city of Beaufort.

Most of the day was used up by the process of transferring all their things to the *Cosmopolitan*, a smaller ship used by the military to deliver mail and supplies. It set sail in the late afternoon and promptly found itself hung up on an oyster-shell bar. No one had checked to discover that the tide was still out.

Susan Walker was fairly choking with indignation. She was used to being surrounded by competent individuals who did their jobs quietly and efficiently. This expedition had become a nightmare of bad management. How on earth would this motley assembly of amateurs ever be able to teach the freed slaves to manage their own affairs, she asked herself. She understood that people who are tired and sick make some bad decisions, but Gideon's Band seemed to have been plagued from the beginning.

Different people see different things. Often the view only reflects their own states of mind. For Austa French, the city of Beaufort was a disastrous disappointment. She had been expecting a cultural oasis in the southern landscape. Instead, she saw streets paved only with sand, gardens full of weeds, once-lovely mansions with gaping windows and doors, piles of broken furniture and smashed bottles.

The Negroes she had come so far to help lounged on the street corners, some obviously inebriated, others engaged in some game being played in the dust, and others ogling the strangers who had just arrived in their midst. Not one of them seemed to offer a welcome, or even to realize that the strangers were a missionary band come to save them. She was vastly disappointed, and an Austa disappointed was an Austa infuriated.

She turned on her husband as the nearest likely target, scowled up at him, and stamped her neatly booted little foot. "You told me there would be a house and servants waiting for us. Where is it?"

"That's what I was promised, my dear. Perhaps our late arrival has discouraged our welcoming committee. Wait right here on the dock. I'll find someone in charge."

He set off optimistically, but it soon became apparent that no one was in charge. A couple of scruffy soldiers finally pointed him at an army officer who just happened to be walking down the street.

"Excuse me. Can you tell me where I might find Mr. William Reynolds, the cotton agent?"

The young major looked a bit doubtful.

"You mean Colonel Reynolds? Your business, sir?"

"I'm the Reverend Mansfield French. I am in charge of escorting a band of fifty-three teachers and missionaries who intend to take over the care and education of these former slaves. We come with the full approval of the United States government, and Mr. Reynolds was supposed to meet us and take us to our accommodations."

"Ah . . . Colonel Reynolds is probably busy with his latest appropriations move. I can't tell you where to find him. He's been rushing through these islands for the last week or so, claiming every plantation and summer home for his own needs. His men are sorting through the houses, gathering furniture and goods left behind by the white planters."

"Good. He must be preparing our residences for us."

"I don't think so. He's been packing everything up and shipping it off to be sold. Seems he needs the cash to pay his slave workers. He's also installing his own cotton agents in every residence that stands vacant. I don't know what you've been promised, but I fear there are no arrangements for you here. The army has problems enough with him and his men trying to drive our companies out of their quarters."

Reverend French rushed to find Edward Pierce. "What's happened here? That officer over there tells me that Mr.

Reynolds is occupying every available house and that there are no quarters left for us."

Of course Pierce was as confused as everyone else, but he did know where General Stevens made his headquarters. "I'll return as quickly as possible. In the meanwhile, see if you can make everyone comfortable here on the dock or in that open area over there under the trees."

"I don't like the sound of this," grumbled Austa from behind her husband's shoulder. "We have nowhere to go? That's preposterous. We're just supposed to sit here and let all those darkies ogle us?"

"I'm sure it won't be long, my dear. And those 'darkies,' as you call them, are the very people you have vowed to help. You might spend some profitable time getting to know them."

"Not under these circumstances, Mansfield. I need to wash my face first."

Susan Walker Tours Beaufort

While Austa French fumed and the rest of Gideon's Band waited for rescue, Miss Susan Walker was investigating the situation on her own. She wandered away from the small assembly and began to explore what appeared to be a relatively busy little street. Soldiers rushed past her on foot or on horseback, intent on their own duties. She, too, noticed the many Negroes who were out and about, but the ones who caught her attention were those who seemed to be going about their business with dispatch.

And not all the houses and storefronts were deserted, she realized. A post office was open, as was a general store and a smithy's workshop. Further along Bay Street, soldiers stood at attention in front of rather prosperous-looking summer homes. Because she had seen Mr. Pierce heading further down that road, she did not follow, not wanting to seem to be interfering.

Instead, she turned toward what must have once been a lovely park. Towering live oaks provided shade from a sun that was growing ever hotter. Those trees themselves were draped in long garlands of the moss that Reverend French had described before their departure. She smiled to herself as she recognized the similarity between the long curly strands and a gentleman's beard. She reached out a hand to feel the texture and then pulled back abruptly as she remembered that the 'no-see-ums' liked to live in the moss. Beautiful from a distance, she decided.

Still Susan Walker saw a lovely little city. When she took a deep breath, the tang of the salt water only sharpened a pervasive perfume. Winter roses and other flowering bushes seemed to fill the landscape. The residents had planted camellias, azaleas, and gardenias, and now they flourished, even if they had not been tended recently. Lilies and magnolias added their own scents, while the flowering tea bushes added a touch of delicacy to what Susan was already seeing as a bouquet put together for her pleasure.

I can be very comfortable here, she told herself. Once we have our own houses, and after we get our schools set up, we'll have the people who need work trim up the gardens. Beaufort is supposed to be the healthiest area in which to live, and the soil looks like it will produce abundant crops. We'll have fish and vegetables and oranges! I've about had enough of living in such close proximity with some of our group, but we'll soon be spread out and on our own. I'm so glad I came.

When Reverend French returned, he brought with him several people who could help solve the housing crisis. At the J. J. Smith House, where General Isaac Ingalls Stevens had set up his command post, French learned that a large townhouse was being saved for the men of the party. The Fripp House, better known as Tidalholm, sat at the east end of town at Number 1 Laurens Street. The neighborhood was known as The Point, for its several blocks of newly constructed mansions were almost entirely surrounded by water.

The general had sent several young lieutenants from his staff to help with the unloading and transporting of luggage. Mrs. Stevens herself had accompanied French back to the dock, where she graciously offered her home to several of the ladies until more suitable quarters could be found for them.

Reverend Solomon Peck was there, too. He had been in Beaufort since January and had already founded his own school for black children. Now he came to the dock to meet his daughter Lizzie, who had traveled with the missionaries to join her father's efforts. Lizzie was young and appeared somewhat frail; Susan Walker had immediately taken her under her protection and care.

"Father, you must meet Miss Walker. She was so kind to me on the voyage. Mr. Pierce didn't want me to come at all, but Miss Walker promised to look out for me. She helped me when I got seasick and made sure I stayed as warm and dry as possible. I'm ever so grateful to her."

"Miss Walker." Peck bowed over her extended hand. "How can I ever thank you enough for taking care of my child. You must come home with us, where you can be comfortable for the next few days."

"I don't want to impose. I'm sure they'll make arrangements for us soon."

"Oh, please, Miss Walker. You must come. Father's told me all about our house here, and I know there will be room. Please?"

Susan hesitated and then, seeing several of the others depart with Mrs. Stevens, she smiled at her young charge. "Of course I'll come, Lizzie. And thank you."

"It's going to be so much fun! Reverend and Mrs. French are coming, too, and Ellen Winsor and Mena Hale. We'll have a regular house party."

Susan felt her spirit begin to wither. She didn't mind sharing accommodations with the younger girls, but the very thought of living in the same house with Austa French made her wish for her own private army tent. Buck up, she warned herself. Not even Austa can be disagreeable all the time. I hope.

Southern Architecture

Reverend Peck lived in one of the more modest summer homes in town. It had suffered some damage in the aftermath of the Battle of Port Royal, but he had refurnished it with whatever he could find. The result was a serviceable, if not entirely comfortable, home. Warmth and food went a long way to soothe spirits of the travelers, and the small house party spent a pleasant couple of days getting to know their surroundings.

Susan Walker immediately recognized Solomon Peck as a valuable resource for her own efforts. Single-handedly he had already accomplished the sort of thing this new group had been sent to do. Susan sensed that the Frenches viewed him as a bit of a rival, but she vowed to make him an ally. She wanted to know whatever it was that had made him a success, so she sought every opportunity to talk with him.

"Would you tell me about Beaufort?" Susan asked one day. "What was life like here before the war? We heard that this was the most cosmopolitan city in all of the South, but I don't see a lot of evidence of that now."

"Well, you have to remember several things. First, before the war, this city was the playground of the wealthiest planters of South Carolina. They had cotton, rice, and tea plantations out on the surrounding marshy islands. Those were staffed by droves of field hands and largely run by slave drivers. The planters themselves lived on the plantations only during certain necessary periods, to oversee the planting of crops and their successful harvest and sale. During the unhealthy summer months, and during the winter holidays, the families all moved to Beaufort for their own social seasons.

"Let me tell you about a typical Beaufort house. The house itself stands on a large lot, frequently has a formal garden, and is oriented to take full advantage of the prevailing southwesterly breezes. The planter families indulged their taste for expensive luxuries by building elaborate mansions, and there were always rivalries to see who could have the most Italian marble and mahogany woodwork installed. Their houses are likely to have very high ceilings, gilded cornices, wainscoting, ceiling medallions, and suspended crystal chandeliers—anything that helps make the rooms feel light and airy. You'll see why that is desirable once we get into the summer months, by the way. Oh, and all of the main rooms have fireplaces for heating during the winter, which creates a whole cluster of chimneys on the roof. Sometimes they, too, are so decorative that they almost look like spires.

Susan sighed. "I suppose for us Northerners, it is really impossible to understand what that pre-war life must have been like. I can't even figure out the living arrangements. There are too many rooms, or not enough, or something. There aren't enough bedrooms for a normal house. And there's no kitchen, just a dining room."

"Ah, now you're talking about Southern architecture. The design probably started out as a simple plantation house, with a central hall, two rooms up and two rooms down. The extensions to the back came later. Most of them have a central hallway, upstairs and down, and the house itself is T-shaped, with the crosspiece in the back. In a house like this, there are two bedrooms upstairs at the front of the house, corresponding to the parlors below. Then, across the back, and above the rear rooms, there's a sleeping porch. A whole family may sleep out there in the summer months."

"I've seen some beautiful houses already. And some of them just seem to sparkle. I haven't been able to figure out what they are made of."

"Well, because of the heat and humidity for a great part of the year, it's best to have thick walls. So builders prefer stone, which we don't have a lot of, or brick, which can be made by the field hands in the off season, or better yet, tabby."

"Tabby? What's that?"

"It's a mixture of sand, crushed oyster shells, lime, and water. Poured into forms, it hardens into an almost indestructible building material. Depending on how many oyster shells are in the mix, it can glisten in the sunlight. It's a bit like building a house out of a beach."

"I've also notice the wide porches."

"Most of our houses have a two-story piazza, frequently extending partially around three sides of the house. The side piazzas have stucco piers or arches left open for ventilation. There may, however, be a formal porch at the front entrance. Greek columns usually support those porches, with Ionic capitals on the first level and Corinthian capitals on the second story. Many houses have two sets of stairs leading up to the main entrance."

"I've noticed that, too. Why do they need two sets of stairs?"

"Hoop skirts." Reverend Peck smiled and waited for her to react.

"What? I can see why the stairs might need to be wider than usual, but . . ."

"Picture a Southern belle in full hoops going up the steps, with a gentleman following behind her. Her ankles are likely to be on display as the hoop swings."

"Oh, for heaven's sakes! You mean they had stairs for the ladies and a separate set for the gentlemen?"

"That's exactly what I mean. Southern through and through."

"All right. I'm ready to believe anything now. Why the two front rooms?"

"A gentlemen's parlor and a ladies' parlor, of course. The ladies' parlor is on the opposite side of the central hallway from the dining room, because the ladies depart from a dinner first, and they don't want the men traipsing through their room to get to their sitting area. The gentlemen linger over brandy and cigars, and then move to their own parlor, which is connected to the dining room. There they can tell ribald stories without offending the gentler souls. The room behind the ladies' parlor, by the way, is usually used for the planter's office, or as a family sitting room"

"All that sounds most refined, but where's the kitchen? You know as well as I that in New England, the kitchen becomes the heart of a home."

"Of course it does. That's the only warm spot much of the year. Here, cold's not all that severe. The bigger problem is fire.

Southerners have a separate cookhouse, out in the slave quarters, which fill the back yard. All food is cooked there and brought into the dining room, so there's no danger of dinner boiling over and burning the whole house down. At most, in the really elegant houses, there may be a separate warming room in the cellar directly below the dining room. Dishes can be kept warm there, and then brought up the back stairs to be served."

"But that arrangement means the family would need a whole staff of servants to cook and deliver meals, and . . . Oh!"

Again, Reverend Peck smiled at Susan. "You just realized one reason why this is a slave-based economy, didn't you?"

"Yes! I guess I did."

"The houses here were staffed by a separate group of hand-picked slaves—the most intelligent, the most domesticated, the most obedient ones they could find. The house slaves had to be absolutely trustworthy and devoted to their owner families, because they were entrusted with the upkeep of the homes while the families were out at the plantations.

"That scheme worked fairly well, when life moved at its normal slow rate, and everyone knew when the master and his family would be in residence. But when the planters and their families fled, when the Union Army marched in and told the slaves they were free, when the world was turned upside down, the scheme fell apart. We are left with the framework of a slave society, but not the wherewithal to use it as it was meant to be used.

"Without slaves, how do you get by?"

"Well, in my case, I didn't need a great deal of cooking, because I didn't plan to entertain. But I had to hire an old black woman to cook for me, in exchange for her room in the old slave quarters. And when I do have company—as now—she brings some of her relatives around to help."

"So you're really still using slave labor?"

"No. I'm paying ex-slaves to work as my employees. There's a huge moral difference."

"All right. Of course there is. But I wonder. Do the slaves see it that way, or do they see you as the new Massa?"

"A good question, and one you will have to answer for yourself. And make no mistake. You fervent abolitionists will have to use the ex-slaves to work for you, too. The way this whole city was structured, you won't find any white workmen. We employ the blacks because there's no other way to get work done. Most of the confusing elements you see now in the city of Beaufort are the direct result of the war. Not all damage is caused by guns. Sometimes the worst damage is caused by the rending of the social fabric."

The Hamilton House

As kind and informative as Reverend Peck was, Susan Walker was not very comfortable at his home. He did his best to furnish food for his guests, but supplies were low and the food nourishing but not particularly flavorful. He had enough plates to go around, but not enough silverware, so they had to pass the few knives around the table and share the spoons. The Peck household was also short on furniture. Susan shared a single bed with Nelly Winsor and Lizzie Peck. Both girls were slender, but the thin straw mattress did not provide much room or comfort. At night they all lay stiff and miserable until sheer exhaustion overcame their reluctance to sleep in these circumstances. Susan rejoiced when the announcement came two days later that the ladies needed to pack their things. Permanent lodgings had been found for them at the Paul Hamilton House. But her relief did not last long.

"Where exactly are we going?" she asked the black driver of the wagon, who was loading her valise along with several others. "Will we be located close to one another?"

"Yas'm" came the drawled reply. "I spects y'all gwine be right close in de Oaks."

"The Oaks? What is that?"

"Dat be Massa Hamilton's summer house. It right nex' do' to Tidalholm, wheres yo' menfolks be livin'."

"But which one of us is going there?"

"Everbuddy gwine dere, Missy."

"But there are twelve of us!"

"Dat right."

No, Susan screamed under her breath. No, no, no. Twelve women under one roof? I cannot imagine it. Some of us are not going to survive. The rest will probably be convicted of murder.

At The Oaks, Nellie at least had a room to herself, and the straw mattress, supported by a bare wood frame, was all for her, provided she did not mind sharing with a few bugs in the straw. There was no bedding, so Susan tore the seam of a petticoat and spread it over the bed as her nod to fastidiousness. Her room also featured a fireplace to keep her warm, and a small porch that looked out over the water. The other amenities, however, were missing. She had only a wooden bench, a packing crate to serve as a stand, and a hollowed-out potato to hold her one candle. A kindly slave brought her an amazing marble-topped mahogany washstand, but did not seem to understand when she asked for a basin and pitcher.

It was, perhaps, the dirt that bothered Susan even more than the bugs. Bugs, she understood. They were tiny, and there was no way to keep them from getting into the house. Mosquito netting was an unthinkable luxury, so everyone accepted the existence of God's littlest creatures as an unavoidable discomfort—a trial and tribulation to test their faith. Dirt, however, was another story. When the ladies first inspected the house that was being offered as their quarters, they agreed that it would not be acceptable until after it had a thorough cleaning.

"The corners of the rooms are positively round," Susan complained. "It looks like someone just swiped a mop across the floor and pushed the dirt into the corners."

"And the cupboards are filthy," Mrs. Johnson said. "I cannot imagine keeping food or other goods in such nasty conditions."

"I see now why there are carpets and mats covering most of the floors," Susan said. "This fine sand gets tracked in from the street and makes wooden floors treacherously slippery. But all the carpets do is collect the sand. They'll have to be taken up and beaten."

At that suggestion, the work force the women had hired to clean the house balked. Carpets were nailed to the floors, they pointed out, and they were never beaten except once a year. And this wasn't the right time.

Susan prowled the house from top to bottom, trying to assimilate and understand what she was seeing. The layout was familiar, thanks to Reverend Peck's lesson on Beaufort architecture, but the condition of the house was dismaying. She had noticed a date carved into the lintel above the front door: "Established 1856." The house was only six years old, but it was already in need of major repairs.

Susan cataloged the damage in her mind. Some of the bedrooms had washrooms attached, but the fittings had been pulled out. Beautiful Italian marble graced the mantels of every fireplace, but it was chipped, and in some places cracked clear through. The fireplaces themselves gaped open without pokers or log-holders or protective screens. Cabinets had missing doors, or large holes where someone had simply chopped a way in. The carved mahogany woodwork sported ugly gouges and missing pieces of trim. The storage areas in the basement were littered with broken bottles—evidence of the once-extensive wine collection that had resided there. A few heavy pieces of furniture remained, like the dining table that could serve sixteen at a sitting—sixteen, that is, if there had been any chairs to go around it.

Only in the back lot, it seemed, was there any show of normal life. There, small Negro children played about in the dirt with the chickens, women were busy in their garden plots, a cow and several goats chewed placidly on the grass, and the elderly sat in the sun talking amongst themselves as they viewed their own portion of this estate. The little cabins that were their homes had open doors and chimneys that offered the promise of a good fire within.

The twelve women assigned to share the Hamilton House did their best to organize their daily lives. None of them could easily accept the idea of using slave labor, and there simply was not enough money to pay a work force on a daily basis. Thus the first task was to divide up the chores. They decided on a rotating schedule, and the women volunteered for their first job. Mrs. French spoke up quickly to claim responsibility for devotions. Two young woman were to procure their food supplies from the Army stores, while three others were brave enough to take on kitchen duty. Two agreed to do the daily dusting and straightening, while others worked on the sorting of clothes and supplies they had brought with them for the slaves.

Susan's task was to do the laundry. She wasn't at all sure how she would go about that, but she wanted to seem cooperative. I'll probably have to ask the slaves for help, she realized, but I'll do as much as I can. With luck, Mr. Pierce will arrange our permanent assignments before we get too dirty. In the meantime, we just all need to be as pleasant as possible and do whatever we can to make the household run smoothly.

Susan and Austa Clash

Again, her optimism was short-lived. Austa French was neither the oldest nor the most prominent member of the household. Susan Walker might well have claimed that title, had she wanted to. But Mrs. French had raised a family of seven children, and she fell comfortably into a matronly role. The only thing she seemed not to understand was that her charges were not children. She and Susan wasted no time before they clashed.

"We will have a prayer meeting in the ladies' parlor every evening before bedtime," Austa announced. "We will pray about the problems we have encountered during the day and we will beseech God to help us succeed in our mission. Then we can all go to bed with our spirits safely resting in his hands."

"Surely you don't mean that as a daily requirement," Susan said.

"Why ever not?"

"Well, some of us are not Methodists, you must realize. Unitarians are not used to such daily public exercises. In fact, we don't mandate worship services much at all."

CAROLYN P. SCHRIBER

"To your discredit, I'm sure," Austa snapped.

"I'm sorry you think so, but the fact remains that some of us may object to such religious rigor. Mandatory worship also carries with it the danger that prayers will become stale or perfunctory—meaningless recitations without sincerity to back them up."

"Are you refusing to attend?"

"No. I'm simply stating a preference for voluntary attendance at these prayer meetings. I think it is fine for you to make such an assembly available. I may participate frequently when I feel the need. I'm simply objecting to you making such decisions for the rest of us."

"My husband will . . ."

"What? Support your demand? Force us to obey? I doubt that he will. He seems quite reasonable to me. We are all very fond of him." Susan was deliberately implying much else beneath that statement, but Austa seemed oblivious to the irony. She simply dismissed Susan's comments with a shrug and a turned back.

It did not take long for the disagreement to erupt again. On Saturday evening, Susan chose to visit a slave church across town, where a friendly black woman had invited her to attend the traditional slave ritual known as a Shout. Susan was eager to witness the ceremony and lingered much later than she had planned. On the way home, the driver of her little cart was detained three times by army patrols that wanted to know what he was doing out and about.

By the time Susan finally reached the Hamilton House she was exhausted, and she intended to go straight to bed. She noticed, however, that several of the men of their party were visiting in the parlor, and she could not just walk past. She took the opportunity to ask Reverend French if he had as yet learned the location of the bed sheets that she had shipped with her things.

"Were those yours?" he asked in surprise. "I'm afraid someone told us they were meant for Mrs. Stevens, so I sent them over there just this afternoon. I'm sorry." He seemed to shrug it off as a minor slip, but to Susan it was a major blow.

"I can just keep sleeping in my petticoat, I suppose." Every eye in the room turned to stare at her outburst.

To cover her embarrassment, Reverend French announced that he would lead a prayer meeting before the group broke up. "Let us pray," he intoned.

Susan did not feel like praying at that moment, but she sat quietly as she often did in church. When the prayer and singing were over, she said said good night and started to leave.

She almost made it to the door before Mrs. French's voice interrupted her passage. "Miss Walker, you have hurt my feelings very much by not kneeling at prayer. I hope that in future you will always do it, and set such an example to the colored people."

Susan held her breath for a long moment, swallowing the impulse to lash back at her. Then she simply smiled and replied very sweetly, "Good night, Mrs. French."

The public rebuke offended more people than Austa French ever expected. Several of the women offered Susan their support, and she learned that the Unitarians at the Fripp House next door had gone home to hold an indignation meeting. Reverend French apologized to them, although not to Susan, and promised to speak privately to his wife about the matter. He realized that such a schism in their numbers did not bode well for the success of the Port Royal Experiment.

Susan Walker had a tendency to be unhappy over every current situation while assuming that around the next corner she would be sure to find utter bliss. She called herself optimistic, but others might have questioned that. Certainly she was seeing the very worst in her short residency at Hamilton House.

"It's not so bad here, Miss Walker," suggested Ellen Winsor. "The work is not difficult, we have plenty to eat, and a houseful of servants to take care of the nastier chores. Mrs. French may be something of a trial at times, but her husband is such a kindly man. I shall miss him when we have to leave here."

"Mrs. French is more than an occasional trial, Nelly. She is a domineering, narrow-minded busybody, with too much time on her hands and a nose that pushes itself into everyone else's business. I find I can hardly stand to be in the same room with her, let alone share her table every day. And the good Reverend French, while unfailingly polite in his own fashion, does tend to be rather rigid in his standards."

"Well, it must be hard on them both, don't you think, to have so many women living under their roof?"

"Of course it is. If I were Catholic, I'd be calling it Purgatory. It certainly seems like punishment. But it's not their house, either, you know. We ended up in this place because it was large enough to hold us all. No one appointed them the arbiters of everything we do. Mrs. French just put herself in charge, and her husband hasn't had the courage to oppose her. That's why I'm so eager to get to our very own plantations."

"Will they be as comfortable as this, do you think?"

"The houses have been stripped, as I understand, but we'll be able to furnish ours again, bit by bit. As the slaves learn that we are there to stay, I think they'll return most of the items they have borrowed for their own use. The best part is that we will be few in number at each plantation. We'll actually have room to spread out and find some privacy when we need it."

A History of Animosity

As Pierce and French set off to make their assignments, Susan drew Reverend Peck aside. "Can you spare a few minutes, sir?"

"For you? Of course. Is there a problem?"

"No. I'm very happy to be here. But I still have so many unanswered questions. And before someone rows me across the river and dumps me into the middle of an abandoned plantation, I need to have a better idea of whom to fear."

"To fear? About what?"

"Well, I look around at all the damage that has occurred here. You've told me what life used to be like in Beaufort, and I see no evidence of it. Everything has been destroyed, and destroyed in a way that suggests violence and people totally out of control. Who did all this?"

"Aha. Not an easy question, that. Perhaps we'd better sit back down. This could be a long discussion. What do you notice first?"

"The absence of furniture, I suppose. Someone appears to have ransacked all the houses."

"Ransacked is not quite the right term. For the removal of the furniture, you need look no further than our esteemed cotton agent, Colonel William Reynolds."

"Why would he do that?"

"Because he can. He has an order, signed by your own Secretary Chase, giving him permission to appropriate anything and everything he needs to get the cotton collected and into Union hands. He's interpreted it very broadly."

"I should say so! How do beds and chairs help with the cotton harvest?"

"First, he says his cotton agents on each plantation need to be comfortable and get their rest, so that they can do a better job. He's established one agent on each plantation and made sure the agent has suitable accommodations and transportation—the best horses, wagons, and anything else he might want. Then he has packed up the furniture and other items not being used and shipped them North to be sold, thus raising funds to pay the ex-slaves to do the work in the fields. Looking at things that way, there's absolutely nothing that he cannot justify taking under his appropriation letter."

"I'm sure that is not what Salmon Chase intended."

"It probably isn't, but that is what his letter says. If Secretary Chase has one failing, it is that he never sees the worst in any man. In some ways, that is an admirable trait, but it's one that unscrupulous people too often take advantage of."

"I'm beginning to understand that."

"There's one more aspect to Reynolds's emptying all the houses. He doesn't want missionaries here. He has every reason to try to make your Gideon's Band of do-gooders uncomfortable—and no reason to try to help you."

"I hate that term—do-gooders, indeed! We're simply doing our Christian duty."

"Yes, of course. Don't shout at me. I'm one of you. But we are all a threat to Reynolds and his goal of maximizing the cotton harvest. He fears we'll convince the slaves that they are truly free and that they will just walk off. He doesn't want them to be able to count and cipher, for fear they will question the paltry salaries he is paying them. And he certainly doesn't want them in school. He needs them in the fields. He is not a supporter of abolition, and he probably never will be. He wants to run all the missionaries and teachers out of the Low Country."

"Well, I, for one, do not intend to let him get away with it. Is he responsible for the wanton destruction as well?"

"No, his goal has never included destruction. If he can find a way to squeeze a penny out of something, he'll do it rather than throwing it away. For senseless destruction, you need to look at the soldiers, and before them, the slaves, and before either of them, the plantation owners themselves."

"Has everyone gone insane, then?"

"Sometimes it does seem that way, doesn't it. Let's start at the beginning. Imagine yourself as part of a well-to-do planter family, with your great plantation producing well, and your townhouse here in Beaufort, where you can relax, throw parties, and enjoy the fruits of slave labor that produces your wealth."

"It's a stretch, but I'll try."

"Now comes the war, and a report that a huge joint military and naval expedition is bearing down on your quiet, luxurious little island. Your defenders are 200 men in a small fort on the coast of Hilton Head, with only a few guns, most of which are incapable of swiveling to aim at a moving target. Here comes the armada—eighty ships, 12,000 soldiers. Your defenders put up a brave fight that lasts only until their guns are blown off of their foundations. Then comes the order to retreat. The few Confederate soldiers who are still alive take flight, heading for the safety of the interior, abandoning the Low Country to its inevitable fate. What do you do?"

"Run, too, I suspect."

"Yes, they grabbed whatever was most valuable to them, pushed family into the nearest conveyance, and followed the flight of the Army. They understood that their beautiful little city was about to be overrun. Would they ever return to those wonderful mansions? There didn't seem much hope of that. Was there anything they could do to fight the enemy? The only hope many of them saw was to do whatever they could to keep their valuables out of the hands of the Yankees.

"We know from stories reliable slaves have told us that the planters destroyed many of their own possessions. There is hardly a working cotton gin in the entire area because the owners jammed the mechanisms and broke the frames before they left. There are houses—Hamilton House was one of them—where someone took a cavalry sword to the basement store rooms and slashed open all the bags of flour, sugar, salt, and coffee, mixing the contents together to render them all useless. They knocked the necks off their wine bottles, too, letting the wine pour onto the floor rather than down the gullet of some Union soldier.

"Others burned, or at least tried to set fire to, their own cotton crops. Planters who had no hope of cashing in on the crop could at least keep it from being turned into Union uniforms. As a matter of fact, we still are getting reports of cotton growers trying to sneak back onto the islands to set fire to their fields. When we brought in people like Reynolds to take charge of the cotton crop, efforts to destroy it increased dramatically."

"So, for the most part, this senseless damage is not the fault of anyone still here? I'm relieved to hear it."

"My story is not finished, I'm afraid. But now you have to imagine yourself a slave, watching your master and mistress running away in terror. They call on a few of your number to drive a wagon or help row a boat, but for the most part, they simply tell you to hide or to follow them as best you can. And then they are gone, and the feared soldiers do not seem to be coming after you. Your world is just quiet and deserted."

"Did the slaves understand that they were free?"

"Doubtful. What does that word mean, anyhow? Free? Free to do what? To try to get to Charleston on their own and find the master who has been beating them for years? Free to go somewhere else? Where? To do what? They were, for the most part, frightened and resentful at being abandoned. Some of the slave-owners had warned their slaves that they should not trust the Yankees—that they meant to ship them all off to someplace nasty, like Cuba."

"Cuba? Why Cuba?"

"I have no idea. But when the Union soldiers arrived, it soon became obvious that they were not trying to capture the slaves. In fact, most of them were trying very hard to ignore them entirely. The few who did talk to the slaves told them what you seem to want them to understand—that they were free. But what did they know about freedom?

"Shortly after those first encounters, bands of slaves roamed through the streets, taking courage from one another, as often happens in mobs. And the Army, I'm afraid, egged them on, as bystanders will. The slaves understood that their masters were gone. And that meant that no one would be giving them their stores for the winter. There would be no yearly distribution of clothing, as usually happened at Christmastime. There were houses full of comfortable chairs, and real spoons rather than oyster shells to eat with. The slaves began helping themselves, and the looting spread from one house to another. A woman who had only one ragged dress eyed those lace and satin curtains and pulled them down. The slaves took the easily-movable objects and carted them back to fill their small, barren quarters."

"So they are partially responsible for the worst of the damage?"

"Only in isolated instances. A few houses with sinks and washstands had been fitted with piping and metal fixtures. The slaves seemed to think anything shiny was silver, and they smashed the sinks to get the metal. In other places slaves found alcohol bottles intact and opened them, with foreseeable results. But, no, for the most part, the slaves took what they thought they could use, and left the other things behind. That's why Hamilton House has a huge dining table but no chairs or dishes to go with it."

"Amazing. And you said the soldiers played a part in this, too. Did they do more than just act as the instigators?"

"Some did, yes. Some did so deliberately, and others were fairly innocent, or naive, about what they were doing. Let me give you one example. I happen to be quite fond of a Pennsylvania regiment that is stationed here. They are God-fearing Presbyterians and have an Army-wide reputation for good behavior. One company of the Roundheads is camped out at the Barnwell plantation at the upper tip of Port Royal

Island. I accompanied their chaplain, Robert Audley Browne, to visit them one day. We found the men of Company C sitting around the living room of the plantation house whittling away at small pieces of ivory. They explained that they were carving new numerals for the fronts of their caps, since the army-issued ones had started to rust and crack."

"Ivory? Where would they get. . ?"

"They had pried it off the keys of the piano."

"Oh, no! How could they?"

"They explained that the piano was already ruined. Someone—undoubtedly the slaves—had stripped all the piano wire from the interior of the case. It was never going to make music again, so they were putting the ivory to good use. Browne rebuked them, of course, but it was too late. If you see a soldier on the street with an ivory numeral on his cap, you can be sure he's a member of Company C, 100th Pennsylvania."

Susan could only shake her head in wonder. "Do I have this straight? The owners wanted to do their part to defeat the enemy by depriving him of the spoils of war. The slaves only took what they needed for their own lives, since no one was taking care of them any longer. The soldiers appropriated other items that were simply going to waste. And the cotton agents took the remaining valuables to sell in order to pay for the labor of slaves. Everyone was to blame."

"Yes, and everyone had an excuse that made perfect sense under the circumstances. So you don't have to fear, my dear. But you may want to remember the lessons, lest you fall into the same sorts of temptations."

"I was just thinking the same thing. I'm sure we'll all be guilty of doing some appropriating of our own as we try to set up our assigned residences. I know I plan to take with me that lovely little marble-topped washstand that a slave brought me the other day. Will that be a sin, Reverend?"

"It's a sign that you are refreshingly human, I think."

Welcome to The Oaks

On Monday afternoon, Pierce arrived at Hamilton House, accompanied by the two ministers, Mansfield French and Solomon Peck. They asked to speak with Susan privately.

"This all seems rather hush-hush, gentlemen. Is there something wrong?"

"We've just been trying to figure out where you can be of the most service to our cause," Pierce said. "Personally, I want to assign you to the Pope plantation on St. Helena Island. That's where I will be making my headquarters. Edward W. Hooper, the stately gentleman from Boston, will be managing the plantation, and he has asked for you, Miss Winsor, and Mrs. Johnson, to work with the slaves there. I heartily approve of that arrangement, because I would also like to be able to take you with me when I go out to visit the plantations where we will have people working. I need someone with a good eye and a head for figures to help me keep track of how each is getting along. You would make the perfect assistant."

"I'm flattered, Mr. Pierce, but you make it sound like there are other possibilities."

"There are, indeed," Reverend Peck spoke up. "Lizzie has told me much about your mathematical abilities, and she speaks so persuasively that I would like to have both you and Miss Winsor as teachers in my school. You know that it is already up and running, and I have applications from at least one hundred perspective students. I need someone who can step in and take over some of the classes immediately."

"No!" Now it was Reverend French who pushed to be heard, and his voice was uncharacteristically harsh. "I certainly don't approve of that arrangement. I respect your school, Solomon, and I admire you for what you are doing. We were happy to bring your daughter to you as one of our group. But I will not have you plundering our best people for your own enterprise. If you need teachers, you will have to find some other way to get them here."

"Then you want me to do as Mr. Pierce asks?" Susan was reluctant to oppose the wishes of the kindly minister who had led their group. She sensed that he could be an ally, and she did not want to take a chance on alienating him.

"If truth be told," French replied, "I'd prefer you to stay at Hamilton House to keep my dear wife in line. No one else in that group of ladies seems to be willing to talk back to her. I love Austa dearly, you must understand, but she does have a tendency to let her enthusiasm get the better of her common sense. You, Miss Walker, are the only one who does not seem intimidated by her, and having you to correct her if she goes too far afield would relieve me of a troublesome worry."

"You each make a good case for your view, but I assume you will at least take my wishes into consideration."

"Of course. That's why we are here."

"Well, then. I came to South Carolina in the belief that a group such as this can be a positive influence on the newly freed slaves. I want to be a part of making that happen. So where do I best fit? I suppose Reverend French's request makes some use of my diplomatic skills, but riding herd on Austa French is not my idea of helping solve the problems of slavery. I have run my own school at one time. That's true. But I was an administrator, not a teacher. I have no idea how I would function in a classroom, Reverend Peck. You have more confidence in me than I have in myself in that regard. I'm a businesswoman and a politician. So use me where I can make the most of my own talents."

Once she stated the matter in that fashion, the outcome was clear. "Go and pack your things, my dear. Mr. Hooper will be ready in the morning to take you three ladies across the river to the Pope plantation."

⌒⤫⌒

Susan's initial optimism was short-lived. The boat ride across the Beaufort River was pleasant enough, and they found a warm welcome from a traveling companion, Mr. Frederick A. Eustis, who was now superintendent of a nearby plantation. He took the small party home with him for a roast beef dinner before sending them on their way toward The Oaks.

"I'm finding this very confusing. We're leaving The Oaks and traveling to The Oaks. Not very original names, are they?" Susan commented

Well, remember that you were in the Hamilton House, which is known as The Oaks in the city of Beaufort. But now you are crossing the river to St. Helena Island, and you'll be living at the Pope Plantation, which everyone there calls The

Oaks, too. Both are noticeably surrounded by some of the oldest live oak trees in the Low Country, so the names come naturally.

Susan shook her head at the arguably faulty logic in that statement and then changed the subject. "It doesn't look like your place has been damaged as the others have been," she said.

"Well, you must remember that, while I am a proud member of Gideon's Band, I am also the owner of this land. I inherited the plantation from my mother-in-law before the war broke out. The slaves here know me and they knew I was coming back, so they have been careful caretakers. Things are a bit dilapidated, but at least the cotton agents weren't able to declare the place abandoned so they could strip it of its valuables."

"Are you trying to warn us that The Oaks has not faired so well?"

"I'm afraid it hasn't. The cotton agent who has been running The Oaks is a Mr. Whiting, and he is a somewhat selfish and unscrupulous man. You weren't able to come over here until now because he was still using the whole house. He would not vacate your portion of it until he was sure that every valuable item had been packed up and removed to his side of the house. You're going to be living in fairly difficult circumstances for quite a while."

Susan's much-hoped-for privacy was not to be. She and Miss Winsor had a single bed to share, while Mrs. Johnson had a separate room but no furniture at all. Susan brought her marble-topped washstand upstairs and placed it in the little washroom off their bedroom, commenting ruefully on how silly it looked in that empty space. "If our slaves bring us back a few things, I hope they include a basin and pitcher, so we can actually use the stand."

The bed, too, proved to be a disappointment. No sooner had they extinguished their single candle than they began to realize they were not alone in the bed. Susan struck a match and even that tiny flame revealed a swarm of bedbugs crawling in and out of every crack in the bedframe. Squealing in disgust, they pulled the thin mattress onto the floor and lay there awake most of the night, sure that the bugs would find them. In the morning, Susan ordered the first black man she saw to cart the bedframe downstairs and out into the yard.

"If you don't wants dis, ma'am, I be happy fuh use it in my cabin."

"No! It's full of bugs. Burn it. This instant."

"Lawdy," the man mumbled under his breath. "Des folk be as bad as de agent."

"Burn it, I said. And when you're finished, you can find some fresh, clean wood to build me a new bedframe."

"Yes'm, but dere always gwine be bugs."

The Formal Pierce Report

A t the end of May, Edward L. Pierce assembled a small group of his most trusted colleagues to help him draft a final report of the activities of Gideon's Band under his leadership. Among them were Reverend Mansfield French, Edward S. Philbrick, Susan Ware, Reverend Solomon Peck, Edward W. Hooper, and William Channing Gannett. He enjoined them to be brutally honest in their assessments.

"I did not start out as a member of this group, Edward," Reverend Peck reminded him. "Could you start by giving me an overview of how many people you have had and where they were located?"

"I have the figures right here. We began with forty-nine men and twelve women, all of whom were placed in their assignments within two weeks of our arrival. Since then others have arrived, namely, fourteen on March twenty-third, fourteen on April fourteenth, and a few at a later date, making in all seventy-four men and nineteen women. Of the seventy-four men, twenty-four were stationed on Port Royal Island, a few of these doing duty at Beaufort, fifteen on St. Helena, thirteen on Ladies, nine on Edisto, seven on Hilton Head, three on Pinckney, one on Cat and Cane, one on Paris, and one on Daufuskie. A few of the above returned North soon after their arrival, so that the permanent number here at any one time, duly commissioned and in actual service, has not exceeded seventy men and sixteen women. The number at present is sixty-two men and thirteen women."

"Would you have been more successful if your numbers had been larger?"

"No, I don't think so. I didn't want to have too many super-intendents all trying to enforce their own policies."

"Did we come with enough supplies?"

"We have had a large supply of clothing, almost ten thousand dollars worth, but it did not begin to meet the needs of the people here. Their masters had left the Negroes destitute, not having supplied their winter clothing when our forces had arrived, so that both the winter and spring clothing had not been furnished. One unfortunate flaw in our plans was the amount of time it took to get our shipments here. Much of the clothing was donated during the winter months in the north. Contributors tended to send warm clothing. But if it did not arrive until April or May, the blacks had little interest in it. By then they needed more lightweight garments. Beyond that, however, I think our clothing supplies have made a huge difference to the black population. Miss Walker, you have had more experience with this than anyone here. Would you care to comment?"

"Oh, it has produced a most marked change in the general appearance of our people, particularly on Sundays and at the schools. It would have been almost useless to attempt labors for moral or religious instruction without the supplies thus sent to clothe the naked."

Reverend French, who had seldom ventured onto the plantations interrupted. "How were the exchanges handled, Susan? Was this a free dole, or was the clothing sold?"

"If someone who came to us had the ability and desire to pay, we accepted the money, and returned the proceeds to the organization that donated it, with the understanding that it would be reinvested for the same purpose. Most of the clothing was handed over without any money being received. In the case of the sick and disabled it was donated, and in case of those healthy and able to work it has been charged to their account, although without expectation of money to be paid."

"I'm not sure I understand the purpose of that."

""It was thought to be the best course to prevent the laborers from regarding themselves as paupers, and as a possible aid to the Government in case prompt payments for labor should not be made."

"And it worked?"

"Oh, yes, I think so. Our belief that they could eventually pay their account has inspired confidence in the Government. The laborers are working cheerfully, and they now present to the world the example of a well-behaved and self-supporting peasantry of which their country has no reason to be ashamed."

"I'd like to add a word about the number of teachers we have," Mr. Pierce said. "It is to be regretted that more teachers had not been provided. The labor of superintendence at the beginning proved so onerous that several originally intended to be put in charge of schools, were necessarily assigned for the other purpose. Some fifteen persons on an average have been specially occupied with teaching, and of these four were women. Others, having less superintendence to attend to, were able to devote considerable time to teaching at regular hours. Nearly all give some attention to it, more or less according to their opportunity, and their aptitude for the work. Still, it has not been nearly enough to meet the need.

"At present according to the reports, two thousand five hundred persons are being taught on week-days, of whom not far from one-third are adults taught when their work is done. But this does not complete the number occasionally taught on weekdays and at the Sunday-schools. Humane soldiers have aided in the case of their servants and others. Three thousand persons are in all probability receiving more or less instruction in reading on these islands. With an adequate force of teachers this number might be doubled, as it is to be hoped it will be on the coming of autumn. The reports state that very many are now advanced enough so that even if the work should stop here they would still learn to read by themselves. Thus the ability to read the English language has been already so communicated to these people that no matter what military or social vicissitudes may come, this knowledge can never perish from among them.

"The teachers themselves concur. They all report a universal eagerness to learn, which they have not found equaled in white persons, arising both from the desire for knowledge common to all, and the desire to raise their condition, now very strong among these people. One teacher on his first day in school left in the rooms a large alphabet card. The next day he returned to find a mother there teaching her little child of three years to pronounce the first letters of the alphabet she herself learned the day before. The children learn without urging by their parents, and as rapidly as white persons of the same age, often more so, the progress being quickened by the eager desire.

"Another teacher reports that on the first day of her school only three or four knew a part of their letters, and none knew all. In one week seven boys and six girls could read readily words of one syllable, and the following week there were twenty in the same class. The cases of dullness have not exceeded those among the whites. The mulattoes, of whom there is probably not more than five per cent of the entire population on the plantations, are no brighter than the children of pure African blood. In the schools that have been opened for some weeks, the pupils who have regularly attended have passed from the alphabet, and are reading words of one syllable in large and small letters. The lessons have been confined to reading and spelling, except in a few cases where writing has been taught."

"I've found the same thing in my school," Reverend Peck added. "There has been great apparent eagerness to learn among the adults and some have progressed well. They will cover their books with care, each one being anxious to be thus provided, carry them to the fields, studying them at intervals of rest, and asking explanations of the superintendents who happen to come along."

"Do you think the interest will continue once the novelty wears off?" asked Mr. Gannett.

"It is doubtful whether adults over thirty years will pursue an education for their own sake," Mr. Pierce suggested. "But if they encourage the privilege for their children, books and newspapers will be read in Negro houses, and that will inspire others."

"Are the children well-behaved?" Reverend French asked.

Susan Walker spoke up again. "Miss Winsor tells me that while their quickness is apparent, one is struck with their want of discipline. The children have been regarded as belonging to the plantation rather than to a family, and the parents have not been instructed to train their children into thoughtful and orderly habits. It has, therefore, been found not an easy task to make them quiet and attentive at the schools. She sometimes found them difficult."

Edward Philbrick nodded. "Yet, Harriet Ware has told us that the schools have been successful in teaching habits of neatness Children with soiled faces or soiled clothing, when known to have better, have been sent home from the schools, and have returned in better condition."

"I've seen much teaching going on in the churches, too." Mr. Hooper now stepped into the conversation. "The Sabbath-schools have assisted in the work of teaching. Some three hundred persons are present at the church on St. Helena in the morning to be taught. There are other churches where one or two hundred attend. A part of these, perhaps the larger, attend some of the day school, but others come from localities where schools have not been opened. It is fortunate that we can point to the teaching of their children as a proof of our interest in their welfare, and of the new and better life opening before them.

"There is another area we need to consider," Mr. Pierce said. "An effort has been made to promote clean and healthful habits. To that end, weekly cleanings of quarters were enjoined. This effort, where it could be properly made, met with reasonable success. The Negroes, finding that we took an interest in their welfare, acceded cordially, and in many cases their diligence in this was most commendable. As a race, it is a mistake to suppose that they are indisposed to cleanliness. They appear to practice it as much as white people under the same circumstances."

"There are difficulties to obstruct improvements in this respect in our district," Mr. Gannet said. "There has been a scarcity of lime and (except at too high prices) of soap. Their houses are too small, not affording proper apartments for storing their food. They lack glass windows. Besides, some of them are tenements unfit for beasts, without floor or chimneys. One could not ask the occupants to clean such a place. But where the building was decent or reasonably commodious, there was no difficulty in securing the practice of this virtue. Many of these people are examples of tidiness, and on entering their houses one is sometimes witness of rather amusing scenes where a mother is trying the effect of beneficent ablutions on the heads of her children.

"We've been doing well in promoting the religious welfare of these people, too" said Reverend French. "The churches, which were closed when this became a seat of war, have been opened. Among the superintendents there were several persons of clerical education, who have led in public ministrations. The larger part of them are persons of religious experience and profession, who, on the Sabbath, in weekly praise meetings and at funerals, have labored for the consolation of these humble believers."

"And don't forget, we've even protected the livestock," said Mr. Hooper. "With our encouragement the military and naval authorities now forbid the removal of subsistence, forage, mules, horses, oxen, cows, sheep, cattle of any kind, or other property, from the plantations, without the consent of the Special Agent of the Treasury Department or orders from the nearest General Commanding. The superintendents have not been permitted to kill cattle, even for fresh meat, and they have subsisted on their rations, and fish and poultry purchased of the Negroes. Thus we have prevented the deterioration of the estates entrusted to us."

"I'm inordinately proud of what we have accomplished, my friends. The success of the movement, now upon its third month, has exceeded my most sanguine expectations. It has had its peculiar difficulties, and some phases at times, arising from accidental causes, might on a partial view invite doubt, banished however at once by a general survey of what had been done. Already, the high treason of South Carolina has had a sublime compensation, and the end is not yet. The churches that were closed have been opened. No master now stands between these people and the words that the Savior spoke for the consolation of all peoples and all generations. The Gospel is preached in fullness and purity, as it has never before been preached in this territory, even in colonial times." Edward Pierce gave a nod of recognition to the two ministers before he continued.

"The reading of the English language, with more or less system, is being taught to thousands, so that whatever military or political calamities may be in store, this precious knowledge can never more be eradicated. Ideas and habits have been planted, under the growth of which these people are to be fitted for the responsibilities of citizenship, and in equal degree unfitted for any restoration to what they have been. Modes of administration have been commenced, not indeed adapted to an advanced community, but just, paternal, and developing in their character. Industrial results have been reached, which put at rest the often-reiterated assumption that this territory and its products can only be cultivated by slaves. A social problem that has vexed the wisest approaches a solution. The capacity of a race, and the possibility of lifting it to civilization without danger or disorder, even without throwing away the present generation as refuse, are being determined. And thus the way is preparing by which the peace, to follow this war shall be made perpetual.

"Finally, it would seem that upon this narrow theatre, and in these troublous times, God is demonstrating against those who would mystify his plans and thwart his purposes, that in the councils of his infinite wisdom he has predestined no race, not even the African, to the doom of eternal bondage. My report to Secretary Pierce will say exactly that."

Plantation Slaves

The new residents of The Oaks soon organized their lives as best they could. The three women agreed to share their chores much as they had done back at Hamilton House. They would alternate responsibilities twice a month so that no one would be obligated to carry a heavier load than the others. For the first two weeks, Mrs. Johnson assumed responsibility for housekeeping, Miss Winsor was to organize a classroom where they could begin to teach the slaves, and Susan Walker took over the task of visiting the slave quarters and sorting the supplies they had brought with them.

Eighty-seven slaves occupied a row of small cabins on the far side of the plantation. Mr. Pierce went with the ladies to introduce them and show them where things were. All of their supplies had been stored at the Eustis Plantation, in a small building that had once housed the plantation overseer. Susan suggested that most of the supplies remain there, and that they use the building as their distribution point. "It's closer to where the slaves live," she pointed out, "and we won't have to move all these heavy wooden crates."

While she began the first steps to identify the crates that contained their own personal necessities and to sort out the clothing that had been donated, Mrs. Johnson and Miss Winsor began their campaigns to instill an appreciation of cleanliness and learning among the slaves. Nelly Winsor was pleasantly surprised to find that most of the slaves were eager to go to school. They had no understanding that school was only for children. Men, women, the elderly—all flocked around Nelly Winsor when she pulled out a book. The schoolroom was quickly set to rights so that class could begin.

Mrs. Johnson was having a more difficult time convincing the slaves that their tiny cabins needed to be swept out, aired, and whitewashed. She managed to get her way through sheer bribery. No one was going to go to school until the slave cabins were clean. There were some mumblings about how silly it was to sweep a dirt floor, but eventually the work got done.

Whenever Susan grew tired of sorting boxes, she joined in the first trips to visit the surrounding plantations. At the Jenkins Plantation, Susan was particularly horrified at the conditions she found in one small cabin. A woman, heavily pregnant, lay on the only bed. Around her in the dirt played seven children, several of them naked, the others filthy and clad only in rags. All appeared skinny and listless, their bellies distended in the early stages of starvation.

She approached the mother, asking gently, "Can you tell me your name?"

"I be Kate," came the answer.

"Well, Kate, where is your husband?"

The only answer was a shrug.

"You do have a husband?"

"Don know."

"Well, who is the father of all these children?"

"Don know."

"Kate, please listen to me. I'm sure you're not feeling very well, but you must take care of your children. They must be washed and clothed and fed. I'm going to see to it that you get enough food for them, and I'll bring you some clothes for the children. But you must promise that you will wash your children before you dress them in their new clothes. Do you understand?"

"Yes'm."

"Kate?"

"Yes'm, I gwine do dat."

Susan was ready to admit defeat. I surely must have faith, she reminded herself, and Kate must, at least, cover her children. She promises to make her cabin and herself clean and to wash her children before putting on the new clothes. Will she do it? I will see her again.

Two days later, Susan returned to the Jenkins Plantation to check, and learned that Kate had just given birth to a strapping baby boy. The other children were still ragged and dirty, but those hygiene lessons would have to wait a while. Susan could not resist smiling at the baby. "He's our first freeborn black," she exclaimed. "We'll have to name him Edward Pierce, in honor of our leader." She gave no sign that she recognized the presumption of ownership implicit in that statement.

The missionaries set about their work with energy and enthusiasm, but the tasks facing them were far more difficult than they had imagined. The largest plantation on Port Royal Island was Coffin Point. Before the war it had contained over 1100 acres of cotton land and employed some 260 slaves. Edward Pierce had identified it as his headquarters on his first

trip to South Carolina, but he had not counted on the depreda-
tions of the cotton agents.

By the time he returned with his band of missionaries, the
Coffin family home had been ransacked and the outbuildings
turned into slaughterhouses for all the cattle on the east side of
Port Royal Island. Selling meat to the army was a profitable side
business, and the agents practiced it until they had exhausted
the available herds of cattle. Pierce identified the cattle thief as
Colonel William H. Nobles, who had been sent by Secretary
Chase himself to help oversee the cotton crop. Pierce immediately complained to Chase, but relief was slow in coming.

For every complaint about the cotton agents, Colonel
Reynolds was sending off a corresponding message about the
uselessness of the missionaries. Reynolds argued that Gideon's
Band knew nothing about raising crops and were making a
mishmash of their efforts. He gloated over one incident involv-
ing Richard Soule, a sincere young man who had been a class-
mate of Susan's brother Joseph. Soule was the newly appointed
superintendent at Frogmore Plantation, which lay on the far
side of St. Helena Island. In one of his first official acts, he
attempted to invigorate the small herd of cattle he found at
Frogmore by feeding them some seed he discovered in the barn.
Unfortunately it was cottonseed, carefully saved to plant a new
crop.

"What kind of idiot feeds his cotton seed to a cow?"
Reynolds demanded.

At Chaplin's Plantation, which adjoined the Jenkins Place,
the elderly owner was still in residence, and the slaves had continued their usual routines, sure that the rest of the Chaplin
family would return shortly. Pierce sent out two of his men to
take over what seemed to be a smooth operation. But Robert

Smith from New York and James Taylor from Boston had very different views of the nature of their responsibilities. In many ways they reflected the overall differences between Bostonians and New Yorkers. Smith had an evangelical calling to save the souls of the Negroes; Taylor was a fervent Unitarian and abolitionist. They disagreed on almost every move, which made the slaves distrust both of them. And into the void of leadership stepped the cotton agents to discredit them even further.

Pierce was also contributing to the impression that the missionaries were useless by delaying their assignments to their plantations. He wanted to make sure all was in readiness for them, and he refused to delegate any part of that job to others. So able-bodied men and eager teachers wandered the streets of Beaufort looking bored and confused. Soldiers and civilians alike ridiculed them, wondering why they had come and how they could possibly make this bad situation any better.

Within two weeks of her move to The Oaks, Susan was complaining again. She hated her turn at housekeeping, and absolutely refused to have anything to do with cooking or waiting table. "The kitchen is in the very back in the slave quarters, and I cannot bear to think of how dirty it must be," she said. "I can usually eat the food, even knowing where it came from, but I don't want to have to see it being cooked."

She had several slaves to help with the housework and professed to believe that she must work side by side with them. She was, however, unwilling to adapt to any schedule other than her own. She would come downstairs in the morning complaining about how cold her room had been. Even before breakfast, she would order Erric, the slave who helped out in the house, to gather a better supply of firewood. Then she waited impatiently for it, even though she had no intention of starting a fire before dark. She scolded the teenaged girls who worked for them because they gossiped in the warming kitchen rather than washing the dishes, and she repeatedly called them to help with the bed making, not understanding that they were per- . haps busy with another chore. Having slaves, she was discovering, could be more of a nuisance than an advantage.

She was happier when her assigned tasks took her out to the clothing stores, where she might work all by herself for a time. She found some satisfaction in sorting the donated items, stacking them by gender and size so their customers could find what they needed. Even there, however, she could find something to criticize. The clothing donated by New Yorkers, she thought, was of a poorer quality than the items that had come from proper Bostonians. She found old men's suits, dusty from hanging in closets for years, stained dresses, torn children's clothes, and other personal items that she believed no real lady should have to handle.

Susan had some doubts about how the clothing should be distributed. Some former slaves came to the store looking for a free handout. She understood that their former owners had given them clothes twice a year, and many of them seemed to look on the new supplies as simply the same sort of free dole. But doing things just as the slave owners had done them was not a good way of showing the ex-slaves what freedom was all about. Some, of course, brought their meager pennies, saved from what they had earned in the cotton fields, and Susan felt better about selling clothes than giving them away. Still, what was she to do about those who desperately needed clothes for themselves or their children but had no money. In consultation with Mr. Pierce, they came up with a subterfuge that provided the clothes on the spot but made sure the blacks understood that they would owe the store a payment for them when they earned some money. Would they really pay at a later date? Susan was sure they wouldn't, but she hoped the idea of credit would begin to sink into their understanding.

Susan Walker also found her teaching duties frustrating. Her first impression of her pupils was that they were ragged and dirty, but polite, welcoming, and more eager for books than for clothes. She was an educator by training and an abolitionist by conscience, and the abolitionist in her believed that to hand out charity to the blacks would be to deny them their inherent equality. At the same time, she could not ignore the lack of social graces that set them apart from other students she had known. She was encouraged on the one hand by their receptiveness but repelled by their lack of basic hygiene. Soon she was sending at least half of them home from her makeshift classroom each morning to wash their hands and faces and put on clean clothes before she would teach them. Of course that caused such a delay that class was often over before they returned.

Her general discouragement manifested itself in new fears for her own safety. She feared the sunlight on her fair complexion and refused to venture out of doors without an umbrella when it was above 72 degrees. On April 11th, the Union Navy attacked Fort Pulaski at the mouth of the Savannah River. Although the battle was nearly thirty miles away, everyone in the islands could hear the cannons. Susan immediately predicted the worst. She confessed her fears to her diary: "Heavy firing all morning yesterday and commenced again at 10 last evening, still continued till about 2 PM—probably cannonading Fort Pulaski 30 miles distant—so heavy as to shake our house. If Sesech gain, we will hang from the highest tree. I look at these tall pines in the grove near my window and wonder which branch will hold me."

Susan received a shock one evening in April when Mrs. Johnson asked to speak with her privately. She was already tired from a long day in the store, and she had planned to retire as soon as supper was finished. "Whatever it is, Mrs. Johnson, can it wait until morning?"

"No. I'm afraid not. I hadn't wanted to tell you until matters were settled, but now I have learned that I must move quickly."

"To do what?"

"To go home."

"Home? Has something happened there?"

"No. I just need to go home. I hate it here, Susan—the sick smell of the pluff mud, the bugs, the sand that gets into everything, the oppressive atmosphere, the flatness of the ground, the unfamiliar vegetation—I hate every bit of it."

"But you knew this would not be an easy task. And we've only been here a few weeks."

"Please don't try to talk me out of it. I've already submitted our resignations to Mr. Pierce and Secretary Chase, and I've just been waiting for them to make arrangements for our transport."

"You said 'our'?"

"Of course. My sister Mary will return with me. I'm doing this partially for her. You know she has not been well ever since we arrived in South Carolina, and I feel responsible for her. I would never forgive myself if I made her stay her through the coming hot summer and something happened to her as a result."

"So I'm to be left here with even more to do than I have now?" Susan realized that she sounded selfish and petulant, but she could not help her reaction.

"Oh, Susan, please don't be angry. I'm sure Mr. Pierce will find a replacement for me."

"Someone I'll have to train all over again," Susan snapped. "How soon do you leave?"

"I'll be traveling over to the Jenkins Plantation in the morning to help Mary pack her things. We'll be back here tomorrow evening and then we leave the next day for Beaufort and Hilton Head."

"So I don't even get a chance to adjust to the idea."

"You'll cope, Susan. You always do. I wish I could be as competent as you are, but I'm afraid I'm just not cut out to handle the conditions under which we've been living here."

Susan retired to her room in a cloud of resentment. She was well aware of the difficulties under which they had all been laboring, and she could sympathize with some of Mrs. Johnson's despair. A major problem facing the missionaries was their inability to reconcile their relationships with the abandoned slaves and their preconceived abolitionist ideals. For almost every one of the teachers and plantation managers, the goal was to train the blacks for full freedom, equality, and citizenship. Yet, they found themselves cast in the roles abandoned by the former slave owners. Their failure to make the slaves understand the meaning of freedom was frustrating and discouraging. Still, Susan clung to the ray of hope that she could make a difference, and she saw Mrs. Johnson's defection as a failure of her spirit.

She spent the next day sequestered in the storage house. She pried open boxes with a vengeance and shook out garments with a vicious snap. Under normal circumstances, she would have rejoiced that the clothing from Boston was in much better condition than the previous batches from New York. There was also a good supply of children's clothing, which they desperately needed. The cloud under which she labored, however, kept her from being happy with anything she found.

Part Three: Character Crossovers

Even when I'm not aware of it, all my books are connected in some way. *Beyond All Price* contains a scene in which Nellie Chase, the heroine of that book, learned of the arrival of a band of teachers known as the Gideonites. The date was March 1862. Nellie wondered aloud if the new missionaries would be able to counteract the damage being done by the cotton agents and Army recruiters.

As Nellie understood, the major conflict arose between those who saw abandoned South Carolina plantation slaves as free labor to provide cheap cotton for northern markets and those who saw the same plantations as fertile ground for proving that slaves could be educated to full citizenship. The question of which goal was more important fills the pages of *The Road to Frogmore*.

Within a few weeks, Laura Towne, the heroine of *The Road to Frogmore*, joined the Gideonites and faced the same problems that Nellie had encountered. Nellie Chase left South Carolina in July 1862, so she was not around to see whether or not Laura and the Gideonites were ultimately successful. If you are curious, however, *The Road to Frogmore* picks up the story of Laura Towne and answers the question of what would happen if the Army, the cotton agents, and the Gideonites could not find some way to cooperate.

This and other connections between Roundheads and missionaries kept cropping up. The Gideonite Solomon Peck was invited to preach to the Roundheads. General Hunter's attempt to free the abandoned slaves had repercussions at the Leverett House as well as on St. Helena Island. The theft of a Confederate boat by a local slave delighted both groups. And eventually the first Beaufort experiments at inducting former slaves into the Union Army resulted in the formation of several black regiments at Port Royal.

None of that is surprising, of course, since all my books concentrate on South Carolina's Low Country during the Civil War. The problems arise when a story bleeds over from one book to another and distracts the reader from the main plot line. The following selections include some of the Roundhead darlings that fell by the roadside during the trimming of *The Road to Frogmore.*

Solomon Peck and the Roundheads

Reverend Solomon Peck had been in Beaufort since December 1861. Deeply moved by the first reports of the abandoned slaves after the Battle of Port Royal, he had not waited for a vacillating government to decide on a public policy. Neither was he willing to wait until the abolitionists of Boston and New York could form their commissions and find funds to sponsor missionaries for the area. He simply recognized a need and took full responsibility for his own costs.

He boarded a ship entirely on his own, arrived in Beaufort the week before Christmas, and immediately took up his self-assigned duties. Peck had heard of a godly regiment in the area, and he was most curious to see if the rumors were true. Within days he had met Colonel Daniel Leasure, commander of Pennsylvania's Roundhead Regiment. Colonel Leasure had welcomed Peck's arrival and invited him to preach to the regiment.

"It's almost Christmas, and we find ourselves without the services of a chaplain," Leasure explained. "Our own Reverend

Robert Audley Browne lies dangerously ill with the swamp fever he contracted at Hilton Head. Our men have been used to hearing frequent sermons, and they miss him. Would you be willing to fill in?"

"I would be delighted, Colonel. But tell me, are your Roundheads really as godly as they are reported to be?"

"They are, indeed. They come from sturdy Scotch-Irish and Huguenot stock. Many of them claim direct descent from the Scotch Covenanters who once fought under Cromwell. They have been raised in staunchly religious frontier families. They have followed their strong Presbyterian pastors, and almost all believe in the cause of the abolitionists. They believe in equality and will fight for anyone whose liberty is challenged. They have a reputation for being the best-behaved regiment in the Army, so I am justifiably proud of them."

"I look forward to meeting some of them on Sunday."

"You'll meet all of them," Colonel Leasure promised.

True to his word, Leasure led over nine hundred men to the local Presbyterian Church that morning, almost overloading the sanctuary and suspended balconies. They prayed fervently, sang enthusiastically, and drank in the new minister's words. At the end of the service, Leasure asked for a moment to speak to his men. He asked them to take a vote as to whether or not there should be a second service that afternoon. To a man, they raised their hands when asked if they would return at 3:00 PM. Peck was overwhelmed. Surely, he thought, with this kind of fervor, his own mission could be a success.

Solomon began his educational efforts with a class of sixteen black children, none of whom had ever heard of their ABCs. Within weeks, most of the original group had learned to read, and others were clamoring to join the school. He sent for his daughter Lizzie to join him, because he needed another teacher. By the time Gideon's Band arrived in Beaufort, he was juggling almost one hundred students and was training four Negro teachers to help with the youngest children.

Nellie Chase and Austa French

Nellie Chase was one of the first women to have to decide how to handle the problems presented by newly freed slaves. She was already "on the ground," so to speak, when the Gideonites and missionaries arrived in South Carolina. She met the missionaries; she talked with them; she admired some of what they proposed; but their solutions were not hers.

On her very first morning in Beaufort, SC, Nellie had awakened to discover that the house to which she had been assigned came complete with an extensive staff of house slaves. Even more startling was the discovery that the slaves immediately looked to her to take over the position of mistress—running the house and giving them their instructions. That was more than she had expected to take on as a Union Army nurse. The black butler wasted no time in teaching her two lessons: (1) a woman is always in charge of what goes on in a house; men take over as masters only in matters outside of the house, and (2) the slaves were "playing a role" and they expected her to play her own role, too.

So there she was—22 years old, meeting her first Negroes and finding that they were her own slaves—people who expected to wait upon her, to carry out her instructions, and to rely upon her to solve all their problems and provide all their needs. To her credit, Nellie coped beautifully. She learned quickly how to play the role of plantation mistress, but she never gave in to the worst aspects of the situation. She genuinely liked and cared for her slaves. She improved their living conditions and their diets, provided them with gifts to make their lives easier, respected their dignity, cared for their ills with as much concern as she would give to the soldiers of the regiment, and tried to learn more about their African heritage.

In the eyes of the Gideonites, however, she was no better than a Southern woman, taking advantage of the slaves and continuing to consign them to bondage. Nellie could not believe that her choices were wrong. She sensed immediately that this particular group of slaves had a strong attachment to the house and grounds where they worked. Many of them had been there all their lives. Freeing them would have meant uprooting them, and that was something she was unwilling to do. Nellie's solutions, of course, were only temporary expedients. She had no abolitionist background, and she was not thinking in terms of long-range problems. Her choices provide a much-needed foil for the theoretical proposals of the staunch abolitionist ladies.

Shortly after they arrived in Beaufort, the Gideonite ladies turned to General Stevens' wife for advice on where to find a church service.

"Well," she told them, "those lovely Pennsylvania boys next door always go to church. Perhaps theirs would suit you."

"Soldiers?" Austa French was skeptical.

"They're part of the 100th Pennsylvania Regiment. People call them Roundheads because they are such devoted Presbyterians—some of whom even claim to be descended from Oliver Cromwell's men. They've cleaned up the church in town, and their chaplain preaches every Sunday. I often attend there. Why don't I accompany you?"

As the small band of ladies approached the church, they encountered Colonel Leasure himself, with several of his staff officers. He tipped his hat gallantly and let them precede him through the sanctuary door.

"Who's the pretty young girl with them?" Susan Walker asked. "One of their wives, I suppose."

"Oh, no, that's Nellie Chase. You'll have to meet her. She's one of the bright spots in Beaufort. She's the Roundheads' head nurse and headquarters manager. You won't believe how someone that young can keep a dozen jobs flowing at once, but she's a wonder."

"Really. Where'd they find her?"

"I don't know the whole story, but rumor has it that she is related to Salmon P. Chase."

Susan raised an eyebrow. "Then I surely want to meet her. I told Salmon we were coming here, and he never mentioned having a family member in Beaufort."

"Maybe he didn't know." The last was spoken in a whisper as the congregation settled into the first hymn.

When the service was done, the curious missionaries made straight for Nellie. Mrs. Stevens did her best to introduce them all, but Austa French took over the discussion.

"Margaret tells us that you do a wonderful job of managing your regiment's living arrangements. How does someone so young handle such a task?"

"I have a lot of help. Uncle Joe, our butler, really runs the household and manages our slaves. They are used to obeying him, so that's not a problem. I'm learning to obey him, too." She was smiling at her own simplicity.

But Austa French was not smiling. "Your . . . slaves, did you say?"

"Yes. An Episcopal minister who was dearly loved by his entire staff owned the house we occupy. He fled with all the other planters when we arrived, but the slaves still think he'll be coming back, and they are doing their best to keep the house and grounds ready for his return. They're well-trained and work hard, so we are really blessed to have them."

"Slaves?" Austa's voice was cold, her eyes even colder. "Did no one tell you why we are fighting this war? Don't you understand that we are here to free the slaves, not to exploit them?"

"But we're not exploiting them. They want to work." Nellie realized that the conversation was becoming dangerous. She looked around trying to catch Colonel Leasure's attention. She needed someone with a bit more authority to counter the force that was Austa French.

As if he had read her mind, Leasure suddenly appeared at her side. "Ladies. We are honored that you have joined us this morning. Reverend Browne was absolutely in his glory with so many lovely faces in his congregation."

"Don't bother with the flattery," Austa snapped. "We're just learning some interesting things about your regiment. Is it true that you're a slave-owner yourself?"

"Certainly not! What on earth gave you that idea?"

"Well, Miss Chase, here, tells us that your slaves really run the house for her."

"Yes, they do. But not because I own them. They've always worked in the Leverett House. Now we pay them to work for us. They're not being treated as slaves. They are Army employees."

"Do they live in the same quarters as they always have? Do they do the same jobs they had before you arrived?"

"Yes, they do, but . . ."

"Then they are still slaves. Miss Chase knows that. She still refers to them as slaves."

"You think they must be freed. It's a lovely phrase, but what does it mean?"

"They must be set free to go wherever they want and become whatever they want to become."

"And just how would you go about having them do that? With what resources? Where would they go? What skills do they have that are marketable in the real world?"

"That's why we are here. We've come to rescue them from people like you. We'll provide the resources and training, just as soon as you give them up."

Daniel Leasure shook his head in frustration. "No, it's not that easy, Mrs. French. You've only just arrived. You haven't had time to assess matters here. You have to understand that their house and the slave yard are all many of these people have ever known. There's a cemetery in the back of our yard. Some of their grandparents and great-grandparents are buried there. This is home. Driving them away would be more cruel than treating them as slaves."

"Which you admit you do."

"No. We don't think of them as slaves. They are servants. We pay them a small salary, feed them, clothe them, and provide lodging for them and their children. I would not stop any one of them from leaving, if they so chose, but they have no desire or reason to leave."

"They must be freed. You have no choice."

"The law of the land says they are still slaves, Mrs. French. President Lincoln is in no hurry to declare emancipation because he recognizes the problems I'm trying to show you. You can't just send some soldiers in and tell these people to go away and be free. They have to be taught what freedom means, and that will take a long time. We're going to put an end to slavery, but first we have a war to win."

Austa pressed her lips together in a tight line. Her chin jerked upward as she spun on her heel and walked away, motioning for her little band of docile women to follow her.

"Whew! She's quite a character. Hardly what I had imagined a missionary to be." Daniel Leasure was watching the receding parade with a mixture of amusement and bewilderment.

"Oh, Colonel Leasure, I'm so sorry I managed to land you in the middle of that discussion."

Nellie was feeling mortified, both by the accusations leveled against the Roundheads and by her own inability to respond. "I've been looking forward to meeting the missionaries, so I just plunged ahead talking about our . . . uh, our staff . . . without thinking. I've been hoping the ladies would help me set up a school for those who want to learn to read. I suppose I've ruined that chance now."

"No matter. You wouldn't want Maudie and little Glory exposed to a classroom run by that woman, would you?"

Nellie giggled in spite of herself. "No, I suppose not. And maybe the others aren't quite so bad when they are not with the imperious Mrs. French."

"Perhaps we're about to find out. Look, Mrs. Stevens is waiting for us to catch up with her."

"I wanted to apologize, Daniel," Mrs. Stevens said. "I was responsible for bringing that bunch to your service, but I had no idea someone would cause such a scene."

"No damage done, Margaret, and no need for an apology. The good Mrs. French is not exactly the kind of woman with whom I would want to spend time, but she didn't upset me. Is she that outspoken all the time?"

"I'm afraid she is. You really have no idea. Imagine having twelve of those women living under your own roof."

"They're all staying with you?"

"Only temporarily, I hope. Their menfolk are out surveying the abandoned plantations on Ladies Island and St. Helena Island. They hope to establish small groups of missionaries at each available plantation so that they can begin to fulfill their mission. I'm hopeful that by the end of the week, these women will have their own places to run and criticize."

Bessie Talks about the Big Shoot

Colonel Leasure and Mrs. Stevens both seemed able to dismiss the altercation in front of the church, but the memory still rankled in Nellie's mind. Later that afternoon, she wandered out to the slave yard, hoping to visit with some of the slave women she now counted as friends. She found Bessie, the cook, puttering in the kitchen house.

"Are you busy, Bessie? Do you have a few minutes to talk?"

"Sho nuf, Miss Nellie. You sits yoself down here at de table and I be puttin some water on de boil."

"I don't want to interrupt your work."

"I jist be stirrin up some benne crackers fuh de chillins. You kin watch and sample dem fuh me."

"I'd love to. But I'd also like to ask you some questions. Do you mind?"

"Dat depen on what you gwine ask."

Will you tell me about the day of the Port Royal invasion?"

"De Big Shoot? Oh, dat were a day! Neber seen de Revend an his family so riled up. Dey was packin trunks an stuffin tings into boxes all higgledy-piggledy. Dey keep callin fuh de wagon fuh get itself harnessed and ready fuh go. Massa try fuh explain dat we were all gwine to Charleston, but it sho dint look to me like dere gwine be room for any black folk in dat wagon."

"Did they tell you to pack your things?"

"No, missus. Slaves don have tings."

Nellie stared at her in surprise. "Of course you have things. I've seen your quarters upstairs."

"But Massa neber did, and not Missus Leverett, nedder. Dey jist assumes dat we be part of dere own possessions."

"But they asked you to go along?"

"Not special-like. I member Massa askin where Samuel be, cause he want him fuh drive de wagon."

"And where was he? Did he drive the family to Charleston?"

"No, missus. We knew sumpin turrible gwine happen, and all de men be already gwine fuh hide in de woods. When white folk start fightin each other, black folk know fuh git outta da way."

Nellie smiled at the irrefutable logic of that statement. "And you? Did you go to the woods, too?"

"All we womens stayed in de yard, but we hid in de upstairs uh de cabins, knowin dat de Massa not be willin fuh climb up after us. We was dat scairt."

"So they left you behind."

"Yes'm. When de packin up were finished, de family jist jumped in de wagon and beat dem horses sumpfin fierce fuh get dem fuh run. I doesn't think dey even membered we was still here."

"And nobody ever came back for you, not even to check to see if you were all right?"

"No, missus. Dey's jist dun gone."

"Once the family left, what did you do? Were you still scared?"

"We wuz all scairt. We cud hear dose big guns gwine boom one after de other. An pretty soon slaves from other houses be runnin in de streets shoutin dat we be free at last."

"That must have made you happy."

"Happy? No, missus, I not be happy at all. What we gwine do ifn we be free? Massa took all der tings an all de food, too. We dint hab no money, no horses, no nuttin fuh take care of us. We women was jist scairt. An de menfolk was still off somewhere in de woods. Soldiers or robbers gwine come bustin in on us and kill us, sho nuf."

"But . . ."

"Dat be nuf talk fuh now. I don wants fuh tink about dat Big Shoot no more."

Bessie turned her back on Nellie, signaling with a wave of her hand that it was time for her to go.

The Legacy of Slavery Past

Nellie was quiet at dinner that evening. Finally, Colonel Leasure prodded her. "What's troubling you, Nellie? You've been brooding all through dinner."

"I was just thinking about that set-to we had with Austa French a few days ago, and what it means for our people here. Did you know that Mrs. French came over here yesterday and demanded to talk to our slaves?"

"No, I didn't. And I don't much like the idea. I hope you stopped her."

"It wasn't I who answered the door. It was Uncle Bob. But I gather he solved the problem quite handily. He just told her there weren't any slaves here and shut the door in her face."

"Oh, dear. That must have upset her."

"I hear she made a little scene on the front veranda before she left. I also expect she'll be back. She's not the type to give up easily."

Daniel Leasure sighed and shook his head. "I'm remembering a discussion we had about this when my wife was here."

"I remember, too. You said that the cotton agents were making plans to turn the plantations into self-governing smaller farms. That the slaves would be given their own land, and the agents would be there to guide them as they made the transition from slave to free men."

"Yes, and I predicted that while the cotton agents worked on the immediate employment needs of the Negro, the missionaries would concentrate on more long-range efforts to spread education and traditional Christianity among them."

"Do you still believe that?"

"I'm not sure. You'll remember that Isabel raised the question of what would happen if the separate groups could not agree about what needs to be done. I suggested that if that happened, we'd all need to stay out of the way. I just didn't expect to have to duck so soon."

"There's no question that some of these missionaries are quite abrasive in their approach. But it also seems to me that no one has thought to ask the slaves what they want."

"They probably haven't. But are you assuming that all the slaves are going to agree on what they need?"

"Well, ours seem to. When I took Mrs. Leasure on a tour of the slave yard, she got the same answers over and over again when she asked our people if they wanted to learn to read, if they wanted their freedom, if they wanted to go out and make a better life for themselves. They all wondered what gave her such ideas. I remember Bessie's answer: 'I believes de bes life is jist stayin where you be planted and doin you best right dere.'"

"We've been fortunate in our relationship with the Negroes here," Leasure said. "I do worry what will become of them when we leave."

"Leave? Have orders arrived for our deployment?"

"No yet, but rumors are flying. There's something big in the works."

⌁

When Colonel Leasure received orders to be ready to move out on April 10th, no one knew for sure where the Roundheads might be heading. Some thought they would go to Tybee Island for the attack on Fort Pulaski, while others expected to attack the railroad line that connected the two major cities of the Low Country—Charleston and Savannah. Whatever their destination, the Roundheads were ready.

Up at 5:00 AM on the morning of their departure, they struck camp, packed knapsacks with two days' worth of cooked rations and forty rounds of ammunition, and set out. After a march of about four miles, they set up a new camp in what one soldier described as a beautiful field; they dubbed their new location "Camp Experiment." Off in the distance, some claimed to be able to hear the guns bombarding Fort Pulaski. They were correct.

Back at the Leverett House, however, all had not been so peaceful. As soon as the Roundheads marched down the street, Uncle Bob had assembled the staff to give them their instructions. "It be time to clean de winter outta dis house," he announced. "Bessie, you be in charge uh seein to de carpets and de drapes. Dey all needs to be taken up and beat ta git de dust out. Den de menfolk gwine take dem up tuh de attic an bring down de muslin curtains and de straw rugs fuh de summer. We also gwine scrub out de kitchens an de laundry whiles dere aint no white folk to be taken care of."

"Why we do dat?" grumbled one of the older women. "When white folk goes marchin off, deys probly not comin back. Who gwine live in dis big house nex?"

"Dey be comin back. Massa Leasure say dey only be gone couple uh days."

"Don tink so," the old woman said to anyone who would listen.

"Mama?" Little Glory tugged urgently on her mother's skirt. "Did Miss Nellie leave, too?"

"Dat be her job, Glory. She be needin fuh go where de soljers go."

"But she dint tell me good-bye." Tears welled in the little girl's eyes. "I tot she love me."

"Hush, Glory. Don' be silly. Miss Nellie be comin back, jis like Unca Bob say."

"How you know?"

"She left all her tings. Even dat lil cat. She be back fuh dem."

"Cotton be still here? Oh, she mus' be scairt, jis like me."

"Maybe you kin find her and love on her a bit."

"What be dat?" One of the men looked around, eyes wide with beginning panic. "I hears de guns shootin."

"Lor have mercy, dey comin agin!"

"Who be comin? De massas?"

"Course not. Where dey be gittin big guns like dat?"

As the echoes of cannon fire bounced off the buildings, Uncle Bob seemed to lose all control of his people. They milled about, stretching their necks to look off into the distance, as if they might see an avenging force of plantation owners marching towards them. Mothers pulled their children into a protective embrace, while young wives urged their husbands to run for the woods again.

"Don let dem take you way," they urged. "You go lay low in de bushes til dis big shoot stop."

"It be de vengeance uh de Lord," old Letitia pronounced. "Dey say we all be free now, but dose guns say difrent. We gwine suffer, jis like before."

"Stop! All of you!" Uncle Bob shouted to be heard over the rising chatter. "We let de first Big Shoot scare us near tuh death, and den dere was no danger after all. Dese guns be even further away. We gots no reason not to believe Massa Leasure when he say dey be comin back in a day or two. De guns not even be firin in the same direction dat de Rounheads went."

"But I be scairt!"

"Free people aint scairt," Uncle Bob pronounced. "We aint slaves no mo an we not sposed fuh acts like it."

"What we be, den, if'n we not be slaves no mo?" Samuel asked.

"We be em-ply-ees uh de govmint."

"An dat govmint gwine protect us?"

"Dat why all dese soldiers be here. Not everyone left wid de Roundheads. I heard Massa Leasure say de Highlanders and de Dirty Dutch regiments still be guardin de town. Now git tuh work, all uh you, an start earnin dat salary de govmint be payin you."

Uncle Bob had been right, as he usually was. After four days, the Roundheads came marching back from Camp Experiment, and life resumed its usual pace. Nellie was relieved that once again her regiment had avoided direct combat. She was even more pleased to see that in their absence the household staff had functioned beautifully on their own. The main house was spotless and ready for summer. Fresh muslin curtains hung at the windows and crisp straw mats had replaced the scratchy wool carpets. "Oh, it feels so good to be home!" she said.

But making such a statement proved premature. Orders that arrived at the end of May made it clear that the Roundheads were moving on for good. Along with several other regiments, they were headed for James Island and a major attempt to take the city of Charleston.

With a heavy heart, Nellie made her way out to the slave yard to bid farewell to the staff who had served her so well. As if they sensed what was about to happen, they assembled around her. "As you may have gathered, the Roundhead Regiment is about to leave Beaufort for good. We are being moved to another island and perhaps to the city of Charleston itself. And after that we're headed to Virginia to take part in another of the war efforts."

"But who gwine take care uh we?" Bessie the Cook demanded.

"I don't know for sure, Bessie, but I think another regiment will take over the Leverett House. It officially belongs to the U. S. Government now, and the generals will want to put it to good use."

"We doesn't want nobody else livin here. How we gwine know they be good to us, like you bin?"

"Does we has fuh stay here after you be gone?" Uncle Bob asked.

Nellie looked at him in surprise. "I thought you wanted to stay here—that this is your home."

"Dat be true nuf," he said, "but white folks keeps sayin we be free now. So can we jis pick up an leave ifn we wants to?"

"Dat right!" one of the stable hands said. "Why we haffa work for de white mens at all—dat what I wants to know."

Nellie realized she still had many lessons to teach, and this was the moment for one of them. Swallowing the emotions that threatened to overcome her, she took control of the slaves, just as she had always been able to do. "No, Micah. I want you to listen to me carefully. You are free from the bondage of slavery. That means no man can own your body, or hurt you without fear of punishment, or sell you as if you were a piece of property. But you have not been freed from all responsibility.

"Just like all people everywhere, if you want to eat, you have to work. You are free to find another boss, if you don't like the one you have, but you will have to work for someone. Otherwise, you will only be free to starve. Do you understand?"

"I spose so. But I fears who be comin here next."

"Let me leave you with my advice. This is your home. Don't leave the Leverett House out of fear. Stay here and protect it and each other as long as it is safe to do so."

"But what if . . ."

"If someone comes to live here and fails to treat you with dignity and respect, there will be other places looking for good people to work for them."

"An hows we sposed to find des new places?"

"The missionaries are one possibility. Or the cotton agents."

"No, missus. We dont trust dem cotton agents. Dey has all de fine clothes and horses and food dat dey been stealin from de peoples. Dey not gwine do nuttin fuh we."

"All right. Let me be more specific. If you need help after we are gone, I want you to seek out one particular missionary lady—Miss Laura Towne."

"Who she be?"

"I knows. Dat be dat plain-lookin' missus what come here one day wid Missus Stevens."

"I members her," little Glory chimed in. "She have dat funny big nose."

"Yes, Glory," Nellie said. "That's the lady I mean. And she does happen to have a rather large nose, I'm afraid. But do you remember what you said to me the day you met her?"

Glory frowned for a moment and then grinned. "I be whisperin' to you dat when she be smilin at me, I forgets to laugh at her nose."

"That's right. Miss Towne is a very wise and kind woman. She's a doctor and a teacher. She lives out at The Oaks on St. Helena Island with Mister Pierce and several other ladies. They have a school there and a clinic, and they always need help with the work on that plantation. If you need help, send word to her. I promise you she will protect you."

Robert Smalls

Robert Smalls had an unusual upbringing for a slave. As the son of a much favored house slave and a never identified white man, little Robert soon became something of a family pet of the Henry McKee family of Beaufort. He grew up in their household, played with their children, and shared their lessons, even though it was illegal to teach a slave to read in South Carolina.

His mother, Lydia, worried that her son would grow up not realizing that in the eyes of the law he was still a slave. Because she wanted him to understand the meaning of slavery, she used to take him down to the Arsenal on Saturday mornings and force him to witness the public slave beatings that took place there. When he became a bit older, she sent him to live for a time with the field slaves on the McKee's Ashland Plantation.

"I'm not gonna hoe cotton for a living, Mama. Why do I have to go live out there?"

"I wants you to understan how mos black folk be livin' dere lives," she told him. "Massa McKee aint always gwine be round fuh protect you, and when you not under he wing, you jis be nother slave to mos folks. You needs to learn fuh survive on de plantation, and you needs fuh feel a few blisters on yo hands. Den ifn you hasta live dat life fuh real, you gwine know how to survive."

In the end, Robert did not stay at Ashland long enough to see his blisters turn into calluses, but he saw enough to convince him that he never wanted to earn his living as a cotton slave. Instead, he appealed to Henry McKee to help him find a job on a boat. The young mulatto slave worked on ships in Charleston Harbor from the time he was twelve.

In many ways, Lydia Smalls' fears for her son were justified. He came to understand the evils of slavery all too well, but he would always have trouble applying the slave label to himself. He knew he was different, and he chose to emphasize that difference. He grew up to be willful and headstrong, firmly believing that he could have whatever he wanted. It was a dangerous attitude for any young man, let alone a South Carolina slave.

On a Christmas Eve impulse in 1856, he married a thirty-three-year-old hotel slave named Hannah Jones. At the age of seventeen, he became a family man, and no one could convince him that he had made a bad decision. By the spring of 1862, the twenty-three-year-old Robert Smalls had two small children to support—a daughter, Elizabeth, and his son and namesake, Robert, Jr., with a third baby on the way.

He was employed on the side-wheeler *Planter*, flagship of Brigadier General Roswell Ripley, deputy commander of all Charleston defenses. This shallow-draft boat, 150 feet long and 46 feet wide, supplied Confederate outposts along the coasts because it could carry heavy loads of armaments through the shallow passages of the Sea Islands.

In the days just prior to Hunter's temporary emancipation proclamation, the captain, C. J. Relyea, and his crew of three whites and eight slaves had been helping to evacuate General Hagood's troops from their base on Cole's Island. Smalls was a better seaman than the ship's captain, and often worked in the wheelhouse, actually steering the ship while the captain struck a swashbuckling pose on the deck. Ripley and Relyea trusted Smalls but gravely under-estimated his intelligence. They freely discussed military orders, strategies, passwords, and secret signals in front of the slaves, wrongly assuming they would not understand or remember what they heard.

"Why does yo always be sittin' on de deck whittlin way at some piece uh wood?" one of the other slaves asked Robert. "Dere be uh good game uh chance gwine on below decks."

"But I can't hear what the Captain is sayin when I'm below deck," Robert explained.

"What yo care what he be sayin?"

" Cause he's telling me how I can steal this ship."

"Gwan wid you. He not be tellin yo nuttin."

"Oh, yes he is, Clem. He just doesn't know it."

"You never gwine steal no ship." Clem shook his head in irritation.

"Yes, I am. And you and the others are going to help me."

'Sho we is! An den maybe we gwine take over de rest uh de world, too."

"I'm serious, Clem. Tonight, when we tie up for the night, meet me back of that old bait shed on the dock, and bring the other members of the crew with you. I have a plan that will set us all free and make us heroes."

Robert Smalls was a persuasive talker, and he soon convinced his fellow slaves that it would not only be possible to steal the ship, it would be easy. "Clem asked me why I'm always whittling on deck," Robert said to the others. "Let me show you. What do you see, Manny?" He held up a small piece of wood.

"Look kinda like a bird."

"It is, indeed, a bird, and if any white man asks, it's a toy for my children. But look closely at the bird's feathers."

"Dey doesn't look much like fedders tuh me," Manny said. "Deys jis a bunch uh lines and squiggles."

"Those squiggles are numbers, and the lines are codes. That little piece of wood contains all the navigation information I need, and all the signals, to let us sail right outta Charleston Harbor."

"Dat be what yo be listnen fuh?"

"That's right. All I need is a crew. Are you with me?"

"I's not so sho," Joshua said. "You steal dis here boat—what you gwine do wid it?"

"I'm gwine give it to the Yankees, and they gwine be so grateful, they' gwine give me whatever I want, for me and for my crew, too."

"But I gots a fambly," Joshua said. "I not gwine leave my chilluns behind. Capn kill dem fuh sho, ifn he tink we done stealed his boat."

"I have a family, too, Josh, one I dearly love. We're gwine take the families with us. I'll make arrangements with each man separately, once you tell me you are in on the plan."

As Smalls kept watching the developments on Cole's Island, he stored away every tidbit he could gather, always looking forward to the day when he could carry out the escape. By May 10, when Hunter announced that he was freeing the slaves, Smalls had his plans well organized. He had convinced the other slaves in the ship's crew, promising them that he could take them, along with their families, safely into Union hands. Smalls' wife and small children were in hiding, along with several other wives, on a boat concealed on a nearby island. Everyone was waiting for the chance to present itself.

On the evening of May 12, the *Planter* docked at Charleston. Captain Relyea and the other white officers left the ship to visit their homes. Gen. Ripley was attending a party in Charleston, leaving Smalls in charge of the ship. Smalls made no move until 3:00 AM. Then he hoisted the Confederate flag and sailed out into the harbor, observing every protocol as it would have been carried out under Relyea's command. The ship made one quick stop to take aboard the five women and three children who were huddled in their small boat and then sailed straight for Fort Sumter.

To further the subterfuge, Smalls put on the captain's braided jacket and trademark straw hat, taking on the captain's jaunty stance on the deck and hoping that the shadows of early dawn would hide the difference in pigmentation. As they passed Fort Sumter, he gave the secret countersign by blowing the whistle in a pre-arranged code. It worked. Waved on by the Officer of the Day, the *Planter* sailed out into the harbor mouth. Then it made a quick turn, hoisted a white flag of truce, and headed straight for the nearest ship in the Union fleet that had been blockading the southern coast ever since November.

When officers of the *U. S. Onward* boarded the smaller ship, Smalls announced proudly, "I have the honor, sir, to present the *Planter*, formerly the flagship of General Ripley . . . I thought these guns might be of some service to Uncle Abe."

He delivered to the Yankees the four cannons that were aboard the *Planter*, but his more important contribution was his knowledge of what the Confederate forces were planning. He knew that on April 16, the Marion Rifles and the Eutaw Battalion had joined the effort to evacuate Cole's Island. They had constructed footbridges across the Stono River as an avenue of escape in case the road was cut off along the Stono to Battery Island. Then, to keep up appearances, they had placed dummy cannon where they had removed the real ones. The flag still flew and the men simulated complete military occupation although there were only about thirty soldiers there. All buildings were prepared for destruction by burning when fired upon by the federal fleet. That news meant that the way was open for Union troops to move onto James Island via the Stono River in preparation for the taking of Charleston itself.

The missionaries at Coffin's Point learned of the story three days later. Slaves and abolitionists alike were thrilled by the story, particularly since several members of the crew, as well as Small's wife Hannah, were from Coffin's Point. Harriet Ware wished she could have been in Beaufort to see the *Planter* steam its way toward Hilton Head. "It must have been magnificent," she mused.

The house slaves, too, wished they could have been a part of the adventure. Harriet Ware reported in one of her letters that when they told one old man about the *Planter*, he exclaimed "Gracious! Zackly, that done beautiful," and he kept on exploding with little comments of delight, "my glory," "gracious," "smartest ting done yet."

For Mr. Philbrick and the other Gideonite leaders, however, Small's actions meant much more than a grand nose-thumbing gesture at the Confederates. Here was proof positive that the Negroes were clever, quick learners, full of initiative, capable of great heroism, and willing to fight for their own freedom.

The abolitionists had been making that claim for years. Robert Smalls embodied their most cherished dreams.

The Reverend Mansfield French wasted no time in exploiting the advantage his cause had gained. He hustled Robert Smalls onto the first ship that could be found headed north, and he personally accompanied him to Washington, D.C. and into the office of Treasury Secretary Salmon P. Chase, where Smalls spent an hour regaling Chase with the story.

Secretary Chase was so impressed that he set in motion a resolution giving General Rufus Saxon permission to recruit Negroes into the United States Army and, after the first announcement of the Emancipation Proclamation on September 22nd, 1862, to create the First South Carolina Volunteers. This regiment would be the first to be manned almost entirely by former slaves, most of whom could neither read nor write, but now stood ready to fight for their own country.

Robert Smalls, himself, followed up his triumph in a singularly middle-class fashion. He had been awarded a prize of $1500 for capturing the Planter and turning it over into Union hands. He used the money to purchase the McKee House on Prince Street in Beaufort, where he had grown up as a slave. He also opened a store on Bay Street and set himself up in business as a grocer.

Incident on Bay Street

A beautiful summer morning tempted Uncle Bob to test out his new status as a free man. He strolled down Bay Street toward town. It was still early, and the sound of birds chattering over their breakfasts was the only accompaniment to his footsteps. Uncle Bob noticed a young girl a block or so ahead of him.

"Another former slave testing her wings," he thought, but he made no effort to catch up with her. Solitude could be a blessing, he knew.

Suddenly a sharp whistle pierced the air. Two soldiers, a bit on the unsteady side and looking as if they had been up all night, stumbled toward the young woman. "Hello, pretty lady."

She kept her head down—a typical slave reaction—and tried to walk away.

"Can't you even say, 'Good morning'?"

She shook her head and kept walking. "You best learn to respect your betters, little lady," he said as he grabbed her arm.

Uncle Bob stopped, unwilling to step into a dangerous confrontation, but also worried about the girl's ability to handle the situation.

"Come on, honey, just give us a little kiss," the other soldier said. "We don't mean you no harm."

"No, please, let me go!"

"Not so fast. You got something we need, and we mean to get us some."

When the two soldiers began to pull her toward the alley, Uncle Bob sprang to her assistance. "Leave her be!" he shouted, catching one of the soldiers from behind.

"Get your filthy hands off me, boy. This is military business."

"No it not, an' I don be yo boy, neither."

"Damn nigger," the other soldier yelled as the girl broke free. The two soldiers hesitated for just a moment, unable to decide which of the slaves to pursue. It was long enough to allow the girl to escape, but Uncle Bob did not react as quickly. Both men turned on him, pummeling him to the ground.

Uncle Bob curled up to protect his vital organs, another well-learned slave response. As he waited for the next blow, another voice called out, "Halt, there! Stop, I say. That's an order, soldier."

The soldiers found themselves lifted to their feet as Army officers stepped in to stop the fight. "Stand up straight and identify yourselves."

"Private Benning, 2nd Maryland Engineers."

"Private Johnson, Sir, same unit."

"Well, men, you have just had the misfortune to do something very stupid in front of your commanding general's son. Let me introduce myself. I am Captain Hazard Stevens, and I assure you my father is going to hear about this disgraceful behavior. In fact, I think he'll hear all the details when he and your colonel have to bail you out of the brig for being drunk and abusive. Sergeant, take these two miscreants to the Arsenal and lock them up for a spell."

At the sound of Captain Stevens' name, Uncle Bob slowly began to uncurl himself. He stood, feeling his cheekbone gingerly and testing his jaw.

"Say, aren't you the slave who ran the house for the Roundheads?"

"Yes, sir, I be Robert Hankins, at your service, sir."

"You're the one who looks like you need service. How do you feel? Are you badly hurt?"

"No, sir, I be fine. How de girl be?"

"What girl?"

"De one what dey gwine drag down de alley when I jumped dem."

"No girl in sight. She must have gotten clean away."

The captain looked down the street and shouted, "Sergeant!" The little procession making its way to the Arsenal stopped.

"Keep an eye out for a young black girl who may be hurt. And add a charge of attempted rape to those two."

Once his heart rate returned to normal, Uncle Bob gave up his plan to explore downtown Beaufort and headed back to the Leverett House. His dignity had suffered more than his body, but he was also badly frightened. If this was what a life of freedom meant, he wasn't at all sure he wanted any part of it. And what would have happened to me if those officers hadn't showed up? he wondered. What if that young girl had been our Maudie?

By the time he reached the house, he had made up his mind. "Maudie! Maybelle! Come out to the cookhouse. We need a fambly meetin." He continued out into the slave yard, where he collared Samuel and dragged him toward the kitchen.

Bessie looked up in surprise as her family trouped in. "What in de worl happen to you?" she asked. "Yo eye nearly swole shut. I gwine put a slab uh beef on it, ifn we had any beef."

"My eye be fine but dis fambly aint. We in danger here. Miss Nellie done warn us dat de time might come when we be needin to go somewheres else. Dat time done come."

Briefly he told them the story of the attack. "Widout de Roundheads an de other good regiments, dere are all sorts uh mean soljers roamin de streets. An' we gots nobody here to protect us. I be worrit bout de girls an de chilluns."

"But where we gwine go?"

"Miss Nellie say to find Miss Laura Towne a' she gwine help us."

"An' where we gwine find dis Miss Towne?"

"I gwine find her. De rest uh you need fuh start packin up you tings, and start closin up de big house."

Just an hour or so later, someone knocked at the front door. Maybelle hurried to answer it, but first she peered out through the side window to be sure those mean soldiers had not followed Uncle Bob home.

"Good afternoon, Maybelle. Do you remember me? I'm Mrs. Stevens from next door, and this is Miss Laura Towne. We've come to . . . "

"Lawdy, Lawdy, Lawdy! It be a miracle!" Maybelle was so overcome that she sat down right there on the floor.

"Here, let me help you," Laura said. "I'm a doctor. Are you all right?"

Maybelle kept shaking her head and waving her arms in the air. "A miracle! Uncle Bob, come see. It be a miracle come true!"

At the sight of her sister on the floor and two strange women in the doorway, Maudie ran screaming for help. Uncle Bob dashed in to see what the commotion was all about.

"Oh, Missus Stevens. Maybelle, get up offn de floor an be polite to our guest."

"But it be a miracle. Dis be dat Miss Towne you be talkin bout. You say you gwine ask her for help an here she be."

It took some time to get the stories all straightened out. Captain Stevens had stopped by his parents' house and told them about the incident on Bay Street. While the general went stomping off to find the commander of the Maryland regiment, Mrs. Stevens had come to see if Uncle Bob was all right. Since Miss Towne had been visiting for the weekend, she had brought her along in case he needed medical treatment.

Laura went right to work, checking his eyes and testing his jaw. "I don't think anything is broken," she assured him, "but you're going to have a black eye for a few days."

"Dat be all right. I be black anyways, so's nobody gwine notice."

Laura laughed. "I must say you're taking this quite well."

"I be a slave fuh all my life up to now. Not de firs time I be beaten."

"But Maybelle said you wanted to ask me for help?"

"Yes'm. I still does. I aint worrit bout me, but I do be worrit bout my fambly. Dis heres gittin ta be a rough place fuh we. When de Roundheads move out, Miss Nellie tol us to find you ifn we needed to move somewheres else."

"And you want to leave here?" Mrs. Stevens asked. "This is such a lovely house, and Nellie always said you were happy here."

"Yes, missus, but now dere be nobody livin here but we, and we aint got nuttin—no work, jis one lil garden plot, no money, an nobody to protect us. We needs a new home."

"How many of you are there?"

"Dere jist be de seven in my fambly, an we be good workers. I runs de house and my sister Bessie do de cookin. Bessie have a son what run de stable, an his wife an her sister do de housework. Den deres Maybelle lil girl Glory, who needs schoolin, and deres my ol mama, Letitia."

"Oh," Mrs. Stevens exclaimed. "Letitia's the one who knows the Bible by heart and tells the stories in the Gullah language, isn't she?"

"Yes'm, dat be her."

"Laura, you must meet her. She will be so much help with your efforts to learn the language. Surely you can find room for them at The Oaks."

"Of course we can. Uncle Bob, you and your family will meet a real need for our household. If you can take over running the house for me, it will give me time to do my real work of doctoring. How soon can you come?"

"We don need much time cause we aint gots much. Kin we comes on Monday?"

"Well, maybe you better give me till Wednesday to fix up a place for you all to live, but I'll be looking forward to your arrival."

Finding a Home

Within days, Uncle Bob had found a crew to row the family and their few possessions across the Beaufort River and then transfer them to a wagon for the trip across Ladies Island to the Eustis Plantation. There Mr. Eustis himself guided them to the bridge across to St. Helena Island and The Oaks.

Laura was waiting for them with barely contained excitement. Their arrival meant many things. First, it was a symbol of her acceptance, and indeed the acceptance of the whole Gideon's Band, by members of the black community. Second, it would provide the household with much needed help and the promise that things would begin to run efficiently rather than in the haphazard fashion of the past. Laura had no doubt that when Uncle Bob ordered a task to be done, it would be done quickly and well. And finally, the Hankins family seemed like the perfect test case to demonstrate to the opponents of the abolitionists that ex-slaves could indeed become useful and productive citizens.

Mr. Hooper had helped her clean out and set up two cabins for the family. One would house Letitia, Bessie, and Uncle Bob. The other was for Maybelle and Samuel, along with Maudie and Glory.

As for the slaves who had been helping out at the Oaks, they were told gently that they now had new supervisors. The two teenage girls who had been trying to help with the cooking were relieved to know that from now on their jobs would be reduced to such chores as washing up. The house staff, too, was ready to give way. Erric, in particular, took to Uncle Bob immediately. He who had sometimes taken all day to find fresh wood for a fire now dashed about to anticipate Uncle Bob's command.

"You know, I think Maybelle was right when she called my arrival on her doorstep a miracle," Laura said one evening after dinner. "She thought I had come to rescue her and her family. Instead, it turns out that these people are going to rescue us."

With the added free time all of them had, Mr. Hooper began to make more regular rounds of the other plantations, and morale improved all around. Laura made the same rounds, carrying a full medical kit and doctoring illnesses and ailments that had gone unattended before. And in the schoolhouse, the teachers now had more time to work with their students.

Everyone seemed delighted with the arrangement, except for one tiny child. Despite the fact that Glory had always said she wanted to go to school, she found the schoolroom threatening and lonely. She was months behind the other children in her lessons, so she usually sat by herself to do her work. The other children were kind to her, but she shrank back, afraid to talk and show everyone how ignorant she was.

Miss Towne found her sitting outside one day under a tree, her knees pulled up so that she could hide her head in her lap. When she gently lifted the child's head, saying, "Look at me, Glory," she saw that her eyes were brimming with tears. She sat down next to the child and pulled her onto her lap. "Can't you tell me why you are so unhappy?"

"I don hab nobody fuh talk to," Glory sobbed.

"The other children all want to be your friend," Ellen said.

"But I wants muh ol frien. I be wantin Tiger."

"Who's that?"

"Tiger, muh cat fro back to de Leverett House. She be muh frien fuh as long as she be livin. She play wid me an sleep wid me on cold nights. I kin tell her tings and she kin keep a secret."

"You mean you just need a cat? Didn't you know we have lots of cats here?"

Glory looked up with wide eyes. "I aint seen none."

"Well, maybe you just haven't been looking in the right spot. Come with me. I have someone special I want you to meet."

Laura Towne took the little girl's hand and led her to the barn. There, behind a bale of hay, she held a finger to her lips and whispered, "Look quietly."

A nest of kittens lay there, all soundly asleep while the mother cat gently cleaned behind their ears. Glory burst into tears on the spot and fell to her knees beside them, her tiny hands clasped tightly against her chest.

"They are just old enough to leave their momma," Laura whispered. "Do you see one you would like for your very own?"

Glory was still holding her breath. Very tentatively, she reached out and pointed a finger at a tiny bundle of striped fur.

"Dat one look just like Tiger," she said. "He even hab de same white paws."

"Then he shall be yours. You go and ask your momma if you can keep him at your cabin."

"Oh, what if she say no?"

"Then I'll keep him for you in the schoolroom. As a matter of fact, he can come to school with you and listen to you as you read. What will you name him?"

"I—I—I tink I be callin he McGuffey. Aint dat de name uh that book I be learnin fuh read in?"

"Yes it is. And I think McGuffey's a perfect name. McGuffey, I think we've found you a home," Laura said. And then under her breath, she murmured, "And you, too, little Glory."

Lottie Forten and Harriet Tubman

Lottie Forten rode through the South Carolina countryside with a contented smile. She had come to the tip of Port Royal Island to visit the camp of the First South Carolina Volunteers, the first successful attempt to turn newly freed slaves into Union soldiers. Here at Camp Saxton, several hundred blacks now marched in precise formation, their uniforms sharp and colorful, their weapons shiny and well maintained. Their white officers, Colonel Thomas Wentworth Higginson, and Dr. Seth Rogers, the chief surgeon, were her old friends from back home in Philadelphia, and she was extraordinarily proud of what they had accomplished in a few short months.

She had been hoping to be hired as a black teacher for the illiterate troops. Dr. Rogers encouraged the idea and General Hunter had been agreeable, but at the last moment, Colonel Higginson had decided that having a female black teacher would allow rumors and gossip to spoil the reputation of his regiment.

This weeklong visit to the camp was something of a consolation prize. Ostensibly she was here to assess the educational needs of the recruits and make recommendations for future assignments. In fact, she and Dr. Rogers had spent most of the time galloping their horses through the blossoming April countryside, visiting abandoned plantations, picking spring bouquets, nibbling on picnic lunches, and pretending the war was far away.

Sometimes their conversations were light-hearted, but now and then, Dr. Rogers used the opportunity to talk about his concerns for the regiment. One of those conversations began when Lottie asked him about the new colored regiment that had recently been formed. The Second South Carolina Volunteers now shared Camp Saxton with the Higginson regiment, although there seemed to be little communication between the two.

"Just who is this Colonel Montgomery, and where did he come from all of a sudden?" she asked.

"Ah, James Montgomery is no upstart, Lottie. He's quite well known in the west. He led a band of Free-State men in Kansas and supported John Brown, even after Brown was captured and accused of being a traitor. He's a fervent abolitionist, although some would call him a religious zealot. His methods are what worry me the most. He's known for being a hothead and using unscrupulous tactics to defeat his enemies."

"How does he get along with Colonel Higginson?" Lottie asked. "General Hunter seems to envision the two regiments working together."

"Like oil and water, I'm afraid. Higginson wants a model army to prove that blacks can be ideal soldiers. Montgomery wants a band of ruffians to help him slash and burn his way through the enemy countryside."

"In sheer numbers, it would seem that Colonel Higginson is winning the contest. He has almost a full and polished regiment, while Montgomery has maybe 150 men, most of them still wearing the raggedy clothes they signed up in."

"And that comparison is telling. One is for show; the other is for action."

Lottie frowned. "For all of Higginson's fussing about what a female teacher would do to the reputation of his men, I was a little surprised last night to notice that Montgomery has a woman acting as his cook. I only saw her from behind, but I noticed her because something about her reminded me of Harriet Tubman."

Dr. Rogers jerked the reins as he whirled to stare at her, and his horse skittered to the side. "Don't make a remark like that even in passing, Lottie."

"Why not? What did I say? The cook looks a little like Miss Tubman. What's wrong with that?" Lottie was shocked at the doctor's strong reaction.

Dr. Rogers did not answer. Instead he led their horses to a clearing in the woods, and helped Lottie to dismount. Checking over his shoulder he led her away from the road and into the middle of the field. Then, speaking in a lowered voice, he explained. "That really was Harriet Tubman, my dear, but no one is supposed to know she is here."

"But why not? She's famous."

"Yes, dangerously so. Where did you meet her, and what do you know about her?"

"Well, I heard about her in Philadelphia, of course. Everyone knew about the brave little escaped slave who kept going back to help all her relatives escape from slavery. She's the heroine of the Underground Railroad. Then right after Emancipation she came to St. Helena Island to learn about our schools for freedmen. She stayed with us for a while and actually cooked for us, not because we hired her but because she said she missed cooking. But I thought . . . after that . . . I thought her work was done and she could settle down in safety."

"Not likely, given her character. Now she's a spy for the U. S. Government."

"A spy!"

"Yes, and who better than a tiny black woman who can move among the shadows without being seen? Who knows every hiding nook and trick in the book?"

"So what's she doing in Montgomery's camp? Is she spying on him?"

"No. Actually she's spying for him. Look, Lottie, you're not supposed to know any of this! And if truth be told, I don't know much, either. I know she's here on orders from General Hunter. She carries a piece of paper that grants her free movement wherever she wants to go. It also entitles her to anything she may ask for. I know she specifically asked to work with Montgomery because they knew each other at the time of the John Brown raid. What they are planning, I have no idea. I understand, though, that South Carolina could be a dangerous place for her if the Confederates could lay hands on her. Camp Saxton seems like a safe place to hide her temporarily because our men don't recognize her. They just think she's the cook. And that's the way Montgomery wants to keep it."

"Oh, I'll reassure her that I won't give her away."

"You'll do nothing of the kind. You won't give any sign that you know her. Do you understand?"

"No, not really, but I'll stay far away from her if that's what you want."

Lottie did not have long to worry about keeping her promise, because by the next day Harriet Tubman was no longer around. No one commented about her disappearance because they couldn't admit she had ever been there. Lottie thought about it now and then, and she worried once in a while about what had happened to Harriet, but there was no way to ask.

May was such a busy month that Lottie had little time to speculate on the unknowable. Since her plans to join the 1st South Carolina Colored Regiment had been quashed, she was moving out to Seaside Plantation to start a new school there. And back at the Oaks, preparations were underway for the wedding of Nelly Winsor and Josiah Fairfield. Lottie had volunteered to handle the decorations at the church, so her head was full of plans for flower arrangements.

Then, on June 2, a horseman galloped into the yard at the Oaks waving a message for Laura Towne. "This is urgent!" he said, handing the sealed paper off to Lottie, who happened to be in the yard. "See to it that Miss Towne gets it immediately."

"Mistaken for a slave again," Lottie grumbled, but she set off for the house.

Laura Towne's forehead wrinkled as she noted that the message came from General Saxton. The two of them were still on rather tenuous ground as far as their friendship was concerned, so she gathered the message was more to do with military business than a personal greeting. Still, the contents surprised her:

> My Dear Miss Towne,
> I urgently need you and your staff to be present in Beaufort tomorrow morning. Please bring as many of your people as you can. I've been asked to make sure that Miss Forten is there as well. We'll meet you at the docks

by 9:00 AM at the latest. You should plan to be occupied most of the day.

Yours,

Gen. Rufus Saxton, Commanding

"I wonder what this is all about," she remarked to Lottie, who was hovering around out of curiosity. "It appears that we shall all be arising very early in the morning. We'll have to cancel all classes for the day, I suppose. Do you have any idea what is going on?"

Lottie shrugged and shook her head. In her experience, a vague summons from an authority figure was never good news, but she could not think of any recent problems that needed attention from a general. "I suppose we'll find out soon enough," she said. "I'll take care of letting the children know they have a day off from school."

Raid on the Combahee

The next morning was delightfully cool, and the teachers from St. Helena enjoyed the short boat ride across the river to Beaufort. As they approached the city, they could see a small crowd gathering at the water's edge, but nothing seemed amiss.

Lottie was delighted to see that Doctor Rogers was there. He greeted her as she stepped off the boat. "Come," he said, "I want you to have a place in the front row. You're going to enjoy this."

Mystified, she followed him through the crowd, noticing that many of Colonel Higginson's men were present. "I don't see Colonel Montgomery anywhere," she said.

"He'll arrive shortly," Doctor Rogers said with a slight knowing smile.

A shout went up from somewhere in the crowd. "Gunboats approaching from the west!"

"From the west? Coming down the river? Are we under attack?"

"No, this is a scheduled arrival."

Lottie stood on tiptoe and strained to see the boats more clearly. "They appear to be loaded down with passengers, and there's someone standing at the prow, but that's all I can make out."

As the gunboats came closer, she caught her breath. "They all appear to be black, but I still don't understand the person at the front of the boat. It's certainly not Colonel Montgomery. It looks more like a small child."

"No, not a child. More like a very tiny lady wearing a turban. Recognize her now?"

"Is it . . . no, it can't be. Miss Tubman?"

"I believe so. Listen now. We'll have an announcement as soon as the boats tie up."

Colonel James Montgomery was the first to disembark. He strode to General Saxton, saluted crisply, and shouted so that all could hear. "Sir, I have the honor to present to you some 750 former slaves, newly liberated from the plantations along the Combahee River through the efforts of the 2nd South Carolina Volunteers under the leadership of Miss Harriet Tubman."

A gasp went up from the crowd and then applause and cheers filled the morning air.

The passengers now poured off the boats and for a while chaos reigned. Saxton had planned well for this moment, however, and his officers soon sorted the newcomers into manageable groups. A hundred or more strong young men had volunteered to join Montgomery's regiment, and a couple of black sergeants soon had them lined up and marching toward a makeshift camp. Miss Tubman bustled about, identifying the elderly and ailing so that Dr. Rogers and his staff could assess their conditions and arrange for their medical needs to be treated in one of the local hospitals. The remaining family units assembled close to the docks. Each group of fifty or so had its own military officer and one of the teacher-missionaries.

General Saxton addressed these groups last. "I have arranged for you to be transferred to St. Helena Island, where your needs will be met. Military rations are already there and will be distributed to each family, along with temporary shelter in the form of tents. As soon as we determine how many houses will be needed, we'll be assigning you to empty dwellings on the island. If we need more room, our Army engineers will provide building materials to help you erect your own new homes. Please tell your leaders about any special skills you may have that can help us build your new community. We'll want to identify the cooks, the carpenters, the farmers, the stable hands, and so forth. Welcome to the United States and freedom!"

At last he turned to Laura Towne. "Sorry to keep you in the dark about all of this, but we wanted to make sure the boats made it back safely before any announcement. I've asked Colonel Montgomery and Miss Tubman to join my staff in the mess tent for a debriefing. Would you and Miss Forten care to join us? I'm sure you must be curious about how all this came about."

James Montgomery opened the meeting by describing Miss Tubman's efforts. "She has been prowling around the interior for the past month with her small band of spies. They infiltrated the plantations, talked to the slaves, and learned where the river had been mined to prevent any invasion. She promised her people that they would be rescued when they heard gunboats blowing their whistles. Yesterday she met my gunboats at the mouth of the Combahee and served as our pilot, guiding us around the Confederate torpedoes and taking us straight to the banks of the richest plantations in the area. But she should describe what happened from there."

Harriet beamed with pride as she stood. She described the scene as slaves dropped whatever they were doing and ran to the banks of the river when they heard the whistles. Some tried to wade out to the boats while others clambered into rowboats. A few overseers tried to hold the slaves back. Others, frightened lest this be a trap, hesitated on the banks.

"I tol' de soljers to take der caps off an' let de people see der wooly heads," she laughed, "but some uh dem slaves stil dint trust us, even if we was black like dem. So I stood on de prow uh de boat an' I sang to em:

Of all the whole creation in the East or in the West,
The glorious Yankee nation is the greatest and the best.
Come along! Come along! don't be alarmed,
Uncle Sam is rich enough to give you all a farm.

"Dat was a song I jist made up 'cause I don't know de Gullah language an' we had trouble unnerstandin' each udder. But dey unnerstood bout Uncle Sam. Dat did de trick an' dey all come on da boats.

"I nebber see such a sight," said Harriet; "we laughed, an' laughed, an' laughed. Here you'd see a woman wid a pail on her head, rice a smokin' in it jus' as she'd taken it from de fire, young one hangin' on behind, one han' roun' her forehead to hold on, 'tother han' diggin' into de rice-pot, eatin' wid all its might; hold of her dress two or three more; down her back a bag wid a pig in it. One woman brought two pigs, a white one an' a black one; we took 'em all on board; named de white pig Beauregard, and de black pig Jeff Davis. Sometimes de women would come wid twins hangin' roun' der necks; 'pears like I nebber see so many twins in my life; bags on der shoulders, baskets on der heads, and young ones taggin' behin', all loaded; pigs squealin', chickens screamin', young ones squallin'." [This is a direct quote from Miss Tubman's own narration of what happened.]

"What about the plantation owners and overseers, Colonel?"

"A few got themselves shot, sir. And we torched the plantation buildings and crops. The bosses who were left were too busy with the fires to make any effort to stop us."

Lottie Forten noticed that Colonel Higginson's jaws tightened at the thought of wanton destruction, no matter whose property was involved. "Was that necessary?" he asked.

"Didn't want to leave valuable crops behind, but we were too full of slaves to transport anything else. And we didn't want those Rebels to think about coming after us. With their plantations burned around their ears, they have no further need for slaves. When you find a bed of snakes, Colonel, you kill them all and destroy their den so they don't bite you again."

To ease the tension, General Saxton offered lunch, and the assembled group made its way to the kitchen tent for filled plates. Laura and Lottie talked with General Saxton over the meal, discussing what additional supplies would be needed to accommodate six hundred new residents of St. Helena Island.

"It's not as bad as the situation was when you dropped 1500 Edisto Island residents on us," Laura said, "but our resources are being more fully utilized now. Our plantations can put many of the former slaves to work, but only if you can guarantee that the government will provide enough money to pay them. We'll need more teachers, too."

"We have no choice but to provide for them," he said.

"I agree, but I can't work miracles. My ability to multiply loaves and fishes is very limited."

"You'll get what you need, one way or another," he promised.

Lottie was sorry not to have had more time to talk with Harriet Tubman, so in a couple of days she made excuses to return to Beaufort for a visit to Camp Saxton. As usual, she was a welcome visitor, but when she asked about Harriet, Doctor Rogers winced.

"She's gone, I'm afraid."

"Gone? Gone where?"

He shrugged. "Nobody knows."

"But what if something has happened to her? She could have been captured by the Confederates, or she could be ill somewhere, or . . ."

"This is the way she operates, Lottie. She is a phantom. She appears where she is needed, and then moves on. She works in the shadows, blending into the background so that no one notices her. She could be anywhere, but she won't be found if she doesn't want to be found."

"I wanted to thank her."

"She neither wants nor needs your thanks. She knows the value of her work, and that's all that matters to her. If you want to show your appreciation, you'll not endanger her by trying to find her."

Carolyn P. Schriber is a retired history professor who has written three previous books on the Civil War in South Carolina: *A Scratch with the Rebels*; the award-winning novel, *Beyond All Price*; and most recently, *The Road to Frogmore*. She also published a short version of these short stories in a Kindle Select edition. She now lives near Memphis with her husband and five loveable but opinionated cats. When she is not engaged in managing a non-profit charity connected with Lions Clubs International, she writes and dreams of further adventures in the Low Country between Charleston and Savannah.

Made in the USA
San Bernardino, CA
16 October 2013